13, rue Thérèse

By Elena Mauli Shapiro

13 rue Thérèse

13, rue Thérèse

a novel

Elena Mauli Shapiro

headline
review

First published in Great Britain in 2011 by
HEADLINE REVIEW
An imprint of HEADLINE PUBLISHING GROUP

1

Cataloguing in Publication Data is available from the British Library

Hardback ISBN 978 0 7553 7422 9

Offset in Bulmer by Avon DataSet Ltd, Bidford-on-Avon, Warwickshire

Printed and bound in Great Britain by
Clays Ltd, St Ives plc

Headline's policy is to use papers that are natural, renewable and recyclable
products and made from wood grown in sustainable forests. The logging and
manufacturing processes are expected to conform to the environmental
regulations of the country of origin.

HEADLINE PUBLISHING GROUP
An Hachette UK Company
338 Euston Road
London NW1 3BH

www.headline.co.uk
www.hachette.co.uk

For Harris

Foreword

When I was a little girl growing up in Paris in the early 1980s, an old woman who lived a few floors up from my apartment died alone. Her name was Louise Brunet. She had no remaining relatives to come fetch her belongings, so the landlord had to clear them all out. He let the other tenants in the building scavenge through her stuff and take home silverware, jewellery, whatever they wanted. My mother salvaged a small box filled with mementos: old love letters from WWI, mesh church gloves, dried flowers, a rosary – many objects worth nothing but memories. This box is the sepulchre of Louise Brunet's heart. The story behind the objects is lost; the objects are now the story. As I have carried this strange box through life and across the world, I have always intended to make a book out of it. This book now exists; you hold it in your hands. The Louise Brunet depicted within it is a fiction; the real Louise Brunet is irretrievable. Still, she gave me the stars. I merely drew the constellations.

NB: This is lyrical authorspeak for "The events and characters depicted herein are fictitious. Any similarity to actual persons, living or dead, is purely coincidental."

13, rue Thérèse

On the Record

*J*osianne's gift is a simple square box, its sides about as long as her forearm. It is about as deep as her hand is wide. The white plastic lid has a quaint red crosshatch pattern on it, like the sort you might see on a tablecloth in a small family-owned restaurant. The box is nothing extraordinary, though its contents have been known to induce fevers. At least, that is one of the effects it had on Josianne when it first came to her—perhaps she decided to pass on her gift as much from a need to get it away from herself as to share it with another. At least, the box let her think she decided.

The first was a Russian physicist, whose face she had liked best when flipping through the files of foreign professors. His photograph called to her. She decided to hide the box in his office for him to find when he arrived and explored his new working space. The box had an odd effect on him, too—or maybe the effect was partially due to her easy laugh, her smooth, deeply red hair, her hazel eyes that changed color so strangely with the light, that had something a touch hazardous in them like a faint electric crackle. The next year, there was a Swiss historian. (The gift always chose to return to her.) Then there was a year when none of the scholars appealed to her, and she left the gift fallow.

At first Josianne thought this year would be the same; she'd taken no special notice of him. He was a foreign professor like all the others in her stack: a piece of paper she would have to enter into a database, assign an office space to, order a library card for. When he wrote to ask her questions about his sojourn in France, he was crisply polite—surprisingly formal for an American. When she entered his curriculum vitae into the system, she typed the words without really seeing them—a scholar in nineteenth-century French literature from a California university. It was only when her automatic fingers copied in one of his side projects—translating the poems of Paul Valéry—that something registered with her. She stopped and looked back up at the top of the page to check the name she had entered, truly reading it for the first time: Trevor Stratton.

A translator, caught in the space between two tongues. Such people tend to come a little bit unglued from the task of trying to convey meaning from one code to the other. The transfer is never safe, the meaning changes in the channel—becomes tinted, adulterated, absurd, stronger. Translating Valéry especially is a peculiar choice: his meaning is quite unstable even in the original French. That Trevor Stratton must be a little strange. Well, at least Josianne hoped so.

Now that she has received the photograph he sent her for his library card—the red one that will grant him access to special collections and original manuscripts—her mind is made up. She likes his face. His eyes are slightly widened in the picture, as if he is startled to find himself captured there. She is convinced that she sees the necessary gleam of yearning in those eyes; she thinks she can help this yearning. She is already fond of the graceful sweeps of gray arcing over each of his ears, contrasting sharply with his otherwise starkly black hair, and his mouth caught in something like the beginning of a smile—whether sheepish or mischievous she isn't quite sure. It must be he is ripe for her gift.

She will give him the office with the tall, useless empty file cabinet in the corner. He will probably not think to open all the drawers and look in them his first day on the premises. But he will, eventually, discover a box tucked all the way into the darkness at the back of the bottom drawer, innocent-looking yet unexpected. How could one see such a thing and then not take a little peek inside?

She wonders what effect it will have on him.

This is the lid on the box:

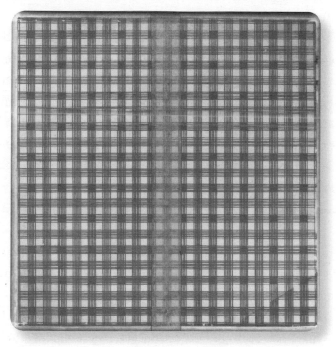

Would you like to open it?

Dear Sir,

Quite by accident, I have found the most fascinating record. I will be sending you scraps of my findings as I extract them—thus you must forgive me if the documentation does not yet make much sense to you. I will send all to you in the order in which I find it, and once I have all the data there is for me to excavate, I will attempt to collate everything into something more cogent. The letters are not in any order. Neither are the photographs. Neither are the coins, the gloves, the cards, nor anything else. It is all quite pell-mell, quite a puzzle.

It has snowed here in Paris, a good fall that layers everything in a lovely sheen of glimmering white. The poor French are utterly routed by this development: it seldom snows here. Traffic is gridlocked; people are stuck places. It is rather funny. I am told that when it snows, generally it is in tiny flakes that melt as soon as they hit the ground. This snow has stuck, and no one knows what to do.

So I am scanning the pieces of the record as I come upon them, and sending copies of the scans to you, should some ill luck befall my notes. Included with this missive are my first findings:

1. a letter asking for a girl's hand in marriage, dated 22 November 1915 (accompanied by my clumsy translation).
2. two photographs of the same man, taken approximately fifty years apart. (These are the largest photographs—

6

they rested on top of all the artifacts. They are approximately six by nine inches, and quite beautifully preserved. The first is dated 26 January 1943. The second is undated, and likely taken in the last decade of the nineteenth century, from the looks and clothes of the fellow in the picture.)

3. a postcard from a father to his daughter from the front lines, dated 12 October 1918.

4. a rosary.

5. a tiny diary with a drawing of roses on the cover, which calls itself "Little Memento Calendar for 1928." (The thing fits in the palm of the hand. I have scanned the cover and a few of the pages.)

6. two calling cards: one for M. & Mme Henri Brunet, and one for Madame Henri Brunet alone. (I have not yet found a photograph of the woman herself. Perhaps I will, but I'm not sure—perhaps she is not much for pictures of herself? Her Christian name is Louise.)

That is all I have to show you for now, but there will be more. I cannot tell you when for sure. I am constantly being sidetracked by other projects. Also, by absurd administrative rigmaroles: the French appear to have a fondness for that! Especially the pretty red-haired secretary, who loves to stamp things, and have me fill them out in triplicate, and make me take them places to be stamped again, and bring them back. On some days this tickles me. On other days, it makes me want to press the palms of both my hands against my ears to keep my brains from spilling out of them.

I am well these days, Sir. As a matter of fact, surprisingly well, considering that all my colleagues appear to be dropping like flies of various flu-like ailments.

I have told no one yet of this record I have found. Surely, someone would then try to steal it from me. Certainly, the French would insist on sending it to Preservation, and I would have to get a thousand things filled out and stamped before I could look at it again. What a nuisance. For now, I exercise my absolute right to be a secretive and quiet researcher—it is delicious and sweet, like hard fruit candy in the mouth.

Well, I will leave you to your work, Sir, before I get too fanciful with my language again. My greetings to you and yours.

Sincerely,

Trevor Stratton

Trevor Stratton

[NB: The envelope is missing from this particular letter, which is a bother—I am not even sure of the name of the addressee. It is one sheet of paper folded in half, to make a small folio. It is so delicate, splitting along its center fold. You can see that the writer was hardly more than a schoolboy; his endearing clumsiness of feeling and his orthographic errors are a testament to this, as is the fact that he has traced lines on the paper in pencil so that he could write neatly, straight across the page, and then attempted to erase them after the ink from his nib dried on the paper.]

Aux Armées, le 22-11-15- 20h30

Mon Cher Oncle.

Depuis bien longtemps j'ai une chose à te dire et aujourd'hui j'ai tout de même te l'annoncer c'est plutôt un secret. Cela part de l'armée dernière, je suis parti au régiment au mois de Septembre en Algérie, j'avais des idées sur une jeune fille, qui depuis, l'amitié que j'avais au début est devenu de l'amour, et quand je suis parti au feu j'avais le cœur bien gros. Mais il faut se résigner et c'est l'idée que j'ai eut. Depuis que je suis au feu je n'est pas cesser de correspondre régulièrement avec. Quand j'ai été en permission j'étais fou de joie mais il a fallu se quitté, et quand au départ pour la

deuxième fois au front, et que c'est toi mon
Cher Oncle qui m'a vu, je n'est pas eu
le temps de t'en parlé, et aujourd'hui je
compte aller en permission pour le nouvel
an et c'est pourquoi que je t'écris car
au mois de janvier je me ferais un plaisir d'appeler, ma fiancée, celle que j'espère
en faire ma femme et la rendre heureuse. Cette jeune fille est Louisette et mon
Cher Oncle c'est aujourd'hui que je te
demande sa main pour le retour de
ce carnage, auquel j'aurais changer
énormément car la guerre fait le carrac-
tère d'un homme, Mon Cher Oncle tu
excuseras si ma demande est brève, mais
je ne sais pas faire de chichi. J'ai
à te dire que Louisette n'en sais rien
car jamais je ne lui ai dit correcte-
ment, ce que je viens de te dire. Mais
je crois que si ma demande est accepté

elle n'en seras qu'heureuse. J'ai travaillé sur le front pour cela, car j'espérais racheter ma faute en étant au régiment et je crois avoir réalisé cette idée.

J'espère Mon Cher Oncle que tu en feras part à Louisette. J'ai appris par Louisette qu'elle avait quitté Malakoff et qu'elle était chez ma Tante Eugénie. J'espère qu'elle seras heureuse chez ma Tante car elle est bien bonne. Je suis toujours en repos et la santé se maintient. Je ne vois plus grand chose à te dire apart qu'en lisant ta réponse seras pour moi un nouveau grand courage.

Je termine en t'embrassant.

Ton neveu qui t'aime et pense à toi

Camille

At the armies, the 22-11-15—20:30

My Dear Uncle,[1]

For a long time now, I have had something to tell you and today I finally dare announce it. It is a bit of a secret. This started last year, when I left for the regiment in Algeria in the month of September. Then, I had designs upon a young girl, and in our correspondence since then, the friendship that we shared in the beginning became love, so that when I left for the front I had a heavy heart. But one must be resigned to such things, so I carried on. Since I have been at the front I have not stopped corresponding regularly with her. When I was on leave, seeing her made me crazy with joy but we had to part once again. I saw you, my Dear Uncle, when leaving for the second time for the front, but I did not have the time to speak to you of this development. Today I count on being granted leave for new year's, and this is why I write you, because in the month of January I would take great pleasure to call my fiancée the one that I hope to make happy as my wife. This young girl is Louisette, and, my Dear Uncle, today I ask for her hand upon my return from this carnage, where I will have changed enormously since war makes the character of a man. My Dear Uncle, you will forgive me if my request is brief, but I do not know how to make a fuss. I have to tell you that Louisette knows nothing of this as I have never properly told

---

1. His punctuation is atrocious (commas everywhere like anxious hiccupping gasps), as is his sentence structure and his spelling. I simply could not render it accurately in my translation. I have tried to help along his poor wording without utterly destroying the flavor of his voice.

12

her what I have just told you. But I believe that if my request is accepted, she would only be happy. I have labored at the front with this happiness in mind. I hoped to redeem my faults by being at the regiment and I believe I have done so. I hope, My Dear Uncle, that you will accept this request and share it with Louisette. I have learned from her that she has left Malakoff for a spell and that she is now at my aunt Eugénic's. I hope she will be happy at my Aunt's as she is so good. I am still at rest and my health maintains itself. I do not have much left to tell you other than that reading your reply will grant me a great new burst of courage.

I finish by embracing you.[2]

Your nephew who loves you and thinks of you, Camille

---

2. The French salutation *je t'embrasse* confuses me each time I hear it. The verb *embrasser* means all of the following: (1) to hug someone; (2) to kiss someone, chastely, as in on the cheek; (3) to kiss someone passionately—what we call a French kiss, of course. I don't know what to make of it: the connotation must always be picked up from context. It makes for a lot of interesting ambiguities. I choose to translate this word with the English *embrace*.

A photograph dated
26 Janvier 1943

THIS MAN HERE, HE is close to the grave. You do not know how you know this; perhaps it is the melancholy weariness in his eyes. Somehow you know he never sees a free France again. He dies of a massive heart attack just a year after this picture is taken. You see him stricken, breaking a sudden sweat, clutching his left arm with his right hand. Moments before, his face had been so placid as he read his newspaper. Look at the face from moments before and try to read the cause of his body's failure—

If you were a romantic, you would say: he died of a broken heart. He was, after all, a widower. His wife died when his daughter was born—in 1896. It must have been a very, very slow broken heart. Maybe it took so long because it kept getting half-mended by the young women he hired to tend to his children.

Or he died of a broken heart because his country was in bondage—though he survived the invasion by nearly four years. Really, morally, he was quite flexible. The situation was not ideal. He didn't necessarily enjoy it, but he never fought it. He was too old. It was no longer any of his business.

He was seventy-three years old. It was just his time. His last name was Victor. His first name is yet to be found in the documentation.

AFTER THE TROOPS MARCH into Paris in June of 1940, he spends an entire month completely drunk. His daughter is concerned. Her husband says: "Leave him alone. This is how he mourns our country."

This condition is unusual for him. He always had an even temperament. He was always a moderate person. Despite his constant state of inebriation, he isn't loud or sloppily emotional. He doesn't say anything that might get him shot. He hardly says anything at all.

The men who used to work with him say his pathetic drunkenness is caused by his recent retirement—he simply doesn't know what to do with himself.

He never explains to anyone the reason for his sudden excess. In July he comes back to himself. He lives a quiet life. He doesn't belligerently look into the German soldier's eyes when he gets asked for his papers on the street, a mere three steps away from the front door of his apartment building. He doesn't belligerently refuse to meet the German soldier's eyes when the soldier looks into his face, scrutinizing him for signs of subversive tendencies. He respects the curfew.

He buys meat on the black market. On the black market, he also buys a delicate pair of sheer stockings with a black seam up the back: a gift for his daughter. She thanks him but doesn't wear them. She says she will save them for a special occasion.

HE KNOWS HIS VISION up close is failing. His work becomes more difficult. Soon he'll have to retire. This frightens him. He would like to be able to work all the time—it would make it easier for him to ignore the rising rumblings of the forthcoming war.

HIS DAUGHTER HAS BEEN trying for years to have a son. She has not been successful in begetting any child, not even a daughter. She cries to him: "I am too old now, I never will. Why didn't I? Am I not a real woman?"

He holds her febrile body against him. He feels her hot face against his neck, moist with tears. "My dear," he says, "be glad you don't have a son. Look at the shape this world is in. Be glad you don't have a son."

Still, he would have wished a son for his daughter, just to make her happy—even though he knows that the grief of losing a child is much keener than the grief of never having him.

HE LOVES HIS WORK, its tiny precise nature. He can get lost in it for hours. He has been doing this work for so many years that his hearing has lost sensitivity to the sound of the drills and sanders. It hardly even registers anymore. When he was young, the noise echoed in his head for hours after he got home. He could hear it as he went to sleep—even when he made love to his wife, so long ago.

THE GREAT WAR IS receding; it is a new decade, and his daughter seems to be taking well to married life. It doesn't escape his notice that the fellow she married looks strikingly like him. The resemblance makes him smile. It isn't uncommon for good girls to marry their fathers.

She babbles joyfully about having a son. She cannot wait to cut up her wedding dress to make baptismal robes for the plump pink baby boy she will push forth from herself, in blood and pain and happiness.

He looks at his daughter's sweet oval face, at the young hope in her dark eyes, and is reminded of his wife. Louise is the only thing he has left.

HE GETS A GREAT price on fifty-seven eight-millimeter pearls from one of his suppliers. Their color is beautiful: a uniform cream that can flatter any complexion. They are also almost perfectly round. Their smooth weight in his hands is a joy to him.

He has one of the women in the shop string them on white silk thread: though his hands are skilled in so many ways, he has never been good with knots. He is a man for metal and stone, for welding and cutting and polishing—a man for intricate patterns in chains of gold and glinting facets on diamonds.

He makes the clasp himself, from white gold. He encrusts it with tiny round diamonds. It is truly a labor of love. He will give his daughter the necklace on her wedding day. She is marrying a fellow that he approves of, who works under him at the shop. The fellow's name is Henri Brunet. He should train him to take over, after he is gone.

His ELDEST CHILD, HIS only son, dies swiftly of the Spanish influenza in December 1918, after surviving the Great War. His life is a disaster. If it weren't for his daughter, he would take the rifle he went to war with, wedge it tightly under his chin, and blow the back of his head off.

HE SERVES IN THE Great War. He is too old for this. This is ridiculous. He is too old for shells and shrapnel and falling men with bloody gore splattering from their shattered skulls—these men who fall and stay there, rotting and dissolving into the noxious earth.

There is an explosion behind him. He ducks from the shower of poisonous mud, covers his head with his arms. Something flies into the back of his neck and gets wedged there. It burns in his flesh. He thinks: it must be a piece of shrapnel. He goes to the doctor. The doctor swabs the site with alcohol, roots around in his muscle with a big pair of flat-ended tweezers. He pulls the thing out and shows it to him.

The thing isn't shrapnel. It's another man's tooth, a man who got blown to bits in the explosion.

"It looks like a canine," the doctor remarks.

He laughs and laughs until tears pour from his eyes. Then he vomits. He will never forget the smell of the alcohol and the needling pain in the meat of his neck as the doctor worked in the back of him.

His son is in the war too. This is ridiculous. The boy is just a child; the hair on his face is still downy.

His daughter is in love with a boy he does not approve of—her own cousin, who is in the war too and writes her torrid letters from the front lines. There are so many things that are ridiculous—he doesn't care what world he has to live in, as long as he never has to go to war again.

HE IS IN THE Paris metro with his son and his daughter, each one holding one of his hands. His love for them often hurts him.

The train pulls into the station with a great squeal. It has five cars: four green ones, and a red one in the middle. His daughter looks up at him and asks: "Papa, why is the first-class car in the middle?"

He has never wondered this before. Children ask the strangest questions. He spontaneously answers: "Well, if the train stalls and gets hit by another train from the back, or if it hits a stalled train from the front, the middle car is the safest. It's to keep society's more valuable members from getting damaged, you see."

This just occurs to him as he says it, and it immediately strikes him as true.

"Papa, that's terrible!" His son looks at him with large outraged eyes, his sense of justice deeply shaken.

He shrugs. "Dear boy, this is the world. This is just the way the world works."

HE TURNS OUT THE first young woman he has hired to tend his children. Though she feels so good, he is afraid he will get her pregnant. Then he would have to marry her. This offends his sense of propriety.

IT'S A CLOUDLESS DAY in the spring of 1896 when his wife gives birth to his second child, a daughter, and dies of complications from the delivery. He names the child Louise. He looks at her tiny flailing limbs and feels utterly lost. He thinks this must be the worst day of his entire life. He is still young.

HE SETS AN OVAL SAPPHIRE into a gold ring. The stone's pure blue color mesmerizes him. The filigree work he has wrought around it is beautiful. His supervisor has spent a great deal of time showing him how to do it. He thinks maybe he is being groomed to take over after his supervisor is gone.

The stone glints darkly at him. He has never been so happy. He will give this ring to his wife to celebrate the birth of their son. It's the first piece of jewelry he's made that he gets to take home instead of selling. He is proud of his labor. He is glad that his wife will wear his work on her body.

HE IS FRIGHTENED the day he gets married. He's pretty sure he loves the girl, but he isn't sure about *till death do us part*. That's a long way away. How is a man to know how much he will love a woman decades from now, after she has grown old and withered, and perhaps mean and bitter?

Today she looks lovely in her white lace. Her oval face has a high flush, and her dark eyes will not meet his. She is a virgin. This makes him nervous. Being with a virgin makes him fumble and flutter also, as if this were his first time. At first, the business of clothing removal is very serious—they don't smile. Then, he somehow manages to get tangled up in his own suspenders. He makes himself laugh with his contortions. His mirth means she is allowed to laugh also, and she does.

"Here, I will help you with these," she says, and she does.

They are naked and free and at the cusp of the rest of their lives: it's like he's starting over, as if he were being born.

THIS MAN THERE, HE is barely more than a boy. He has not even left his father's household. This is his first serious picture, taken alone without his family. His father laughs and says: "The next picture you'll have taken, you'll already have your wife and your children. Enjoy your bachelor life!"

He is excited. He looks forward to the future. Look at his forthright gaze. He has just gotten an apprenticeship making jewelry.

His father is disappointed that the boy will not pursue his studies in law but understands that the boy is good with his hands and wants to do something with them. The boy has always been gifted with tiny work.

His protruding ears are endearing. He is too young to even know that a portrait from a profile or three-quarters perspective would be immensely more flattering. The ears would not stick out so. Eventually, he will figure this out.

If you were a romantic, and you hadn't just been pulled back here through what is to come, you would say: He has his whole life ahead of him—how lucky he is.

A Photograph Undated
(likely taken in the last decade of the nineteenth century)

Un souvenir de ma villégiature

THIS IS A POSTCARD that Louise receives from her father in the last month of the Great War:

Who are these men? You do not recognize any of them. The father is not pictured here. At least, none of these faces looks to you like the face of the man pictured on January 26, 1943, or the same man pictured in the last decade of the nineteenth century.

Still, you gaze at this photo because you cannot help seeing the following:

1. The black dog in the foreground. You know nothing of dogs, but this animal looks to you something like a golden retriever, except dark. Is it an especially courageous breed that is well suited to life in the trenches? You cannot know. Perhaps he is just a mutt—perhaps he is even a she. The dog is indeed a female. The men have called her "Eclat d'obus," but just Eclat for short. An *éclat d'obus* means "shrapnel," literally "shard of shell"; there isn't a single word that means shrapnel in French. The men call the dog this because their time at war has given them a perverse sense of humor: Eclat is the daughter of another dog they had before, this one named Obus—thus Shell begat Shrapnel.

   Obus is dead now; she was blown up on the front lines: both her hind legs exploded clean off, with a great splatter of canine gore. The dog's howls of agony were so terrible that the man nearest her took his revolver out of his holster and immediately shot the animal in the head. He wept then, silently, covering both eyes with his hand. He will never forget the heat of his own forehead cupped in his palm that day. He had not cried for some of his best friends—friends who died right in front of him—friends he did not have the courage to shoot in the face to end their suffering though they begged for it, as they knew the ambulance would not come in time for them.

2. Some of the men are smiling for this picture, just a little. How are they doing that? They are so strong.

3. That mincing fellow in the middle. You can tell just by the jaunty tilt of his cap and the limp wrist on his right leg, crossed tightly over the left—just from looking at this, you can tell the man is queer. If you look at the rocky ground at his feet, you

can imagine how hard it is. You can see the dust and the scuff marks on his shoes. If you let your gaze travel up his body, immediately you see the bindings around his skinny shins. You have to look up what those are called: "puttees," you think is the word.

Can you imagine? The soldiers wear them every day. They cannot be comfortable: certainly, they must be tight. Do they not hinder the blood flow down to the feet? Can the men not feel the pulsing muscles in their legs strain against this constriction when they have to run like hell from something?

In the trenches, they sleep in these. They never take them off, never unwind the bindings. They get used to them because they have to. Did you know—each roll of this bandage around the shin is an incantation, truly a binding ritual, meant to keep the meat on the bone. Each roll around the confined flesh is a prayer: don't fall apart

don't fall apart

no no don't fall apart

please.

You see, all the men in the photograph wear puttees. All the men in the picture are bound, trying to keep themselves together. That is how considerate they are, for the love of God and country and women and the other men—for the love of all that is good and true—they keep themselves together because they have to. They are afraid but they are not cowards.

Also, look at how bulky their coats are, and how every single button is fastened, up to the very last one around the neck; they must have several layers of clothes under there. They must be trying to keep the heat in. These men always suffer from the cold. Every day they suffer from the cold, but still they find time to gather at a pile of rocks. They find time to arrange themselves artfully and stay still for a moment—the moment of picture-taking. It is a moment of companionship; they have brought some of their beloved accoutrements: the dog, and the fellow next to the queer one has his pipe in his hand, and the fellow next to that fellow holds what looks like a roll of papers (maybe he likes to write?). It is a moment of companionship; a loose fist rests on a friend's shoulder; an arm wraps around a friend's knee.

Huddled together, but strong

still for a scrap of time

for this picture

look at it

they want you to.

Still, this picture is a postcard that Louise receives from her father—so why don't you flip it over and look at the message?

It reads:

Col d'Oderon—Alsatian Frontier. On 12-10-18.
    To my beloved little Louisette
    A souvenir of my holiday here.
    Your father who embraces you:
    [Illegible initial] Victor

His signature is very difficult to read. Louise's father apparently likes muddled flourishes. You are not even sure what his first initial is. Is it an L? You will have to pay attention to some of the other documentation to see if you can figure this out.

You are caught by his word *villégiature*. You had to look it up in your desk reference because you'd never run across it before. You thought it meant something like a military campaign, but the clear black type in your book states "holiday, vacation."

Holiday?

Vacation?

It occurs to you: perhaps Louise's father has a strange sense of humor also. He has been to war, too. Why should he be different from all the other men?

THERE WAS A DAY, about two months after this postcard arrived, when the father and daughter almost—

But wait, first let us gaze upon another object, relevant to the forthcoming episode—another souvenir that Louise has left behind in the record. It is an object she was given in childhood to pray with, and she always remembered very well the last time she used it to say

Our Father over and over again. That day she tried to muster up all the scraps of faith she might have in her unbelieving heart, her fingers clutching the beads, attempting so earnestly and so hard to believe that it would be all right, that another boy would not be lost. The war had just ended and another boy would not be lost: it was not necessary.

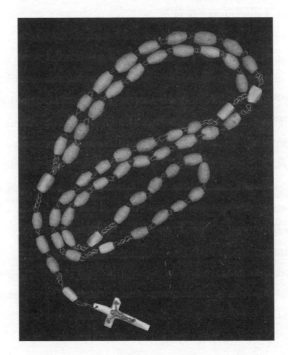

It was a day in December 1918. A weary France had just signed the Armistice. Louise was back at home with her father and her brother. Her father was well and her brother was not. Her brother was in bed delirious with fever, and Louise sat at his side with her wood and mother-of-pearl rosary dangling from her hands, praying for his recovery—oh, if this worked—if he got better, she might per-haps believe a little in a benevolent God, if only for a flicker of time.

Her brother turned slowly on his side. She looked up from her rosary at the soft sound of his body sliding against the clean white sheets. He was facing her, his eyes wide and limpid in his pallid face. His skin always shone now with feverish secretions—he sweated so much that his nightgown was often drenched, stuck to him. At this moment, he looked lucid.

"Do you need anything?" Louise asked.

"Do you see him?" her brother whispered back.

"What?"

"The fellow in the corner of the room—do you see him?"

He did not seem frightened; instead he looked almost conspira-torial, as if they had come upon some unexpected animal in the for-est and he was deciding whether he wanted to spook the animal for fun, or merely stay still and watch it.

Louise looked and saw only an empty wooden chair, bathed by the dimming light of late afternoon.

"He is sitting in the chair," he explained.

It pained her that her brother had clearly gone mad with his ill-ness. She tried to believe that this was not a bad sign. "There is no one in the chair," she said softly.

"Yes, yes—be still and look carefully. There is a man sitting in that chair with his legs crossed and a pad of paper resting on them. He is wearing dark slacks and a white cotton shirt and a blue tie. He is quiet and he is taking notes and he is looking at me."

"Oh, darling, there is no one there—please, come back," Louise said, her eyes filling with tears.

"It's all right. He's not hurting me. He's taking notes on my dying. He is a scholar and such things interest him, you see. He has your rosary in his left hand."

"What?"

"Your rosary, the one you're holding. He has it in his left hand, and when he is not looking at me, he is looking at it."

"That's impossible: I am holding my rosary," she insisted, as if his acknowledgment of this fact would immediately make him well again.

He shrugged. "I know it's impossible, but it is so. He is holding your rosary and oh—now he is looking at you."

Louise flinched as a start of electricity snapped in the pit of her chest when she heard these words, and as the tremor zinged from her solar plexus and down her arms and into her startled hands, she saw a flash of something white above the chair—like the crisp white cotton of the shirt on the man who clearly was not there. She thought she heard a pen scratch a few words on paper. She thought she felt a quizzical gaze run up her body and she opened her mouth to say something, but before any words came out, the feeling of the nonexistent eyes went away and she was sane again.

"He is looking at me again," announced the thin voice from the sickbed. "He looks a little sad. I think he knows I am going to die soon."

"Oh, no—please, don't say that. You're going to get well. I am going to get you another cold compress. Would you like another cold compress?"

Louise's brother smiled weakly and nodded yes, then sank back into his pillow and closed his eyes. It was the strangest episode of his delirium: so quiet and so gentle, not like his other terrified ravings full of shell impacts and screaming exploded soldiers. There was a terrible night where he wheezed and coughed and twisted on the mattress in an agony unbearable to behold, convinced that he was being gassed again.

This day with the peaceful academic taking notes on their unwinding lives in a corner of the room—Louise never forgot it. Her brother died the next day of the Spanish influenza.

Petit calendrier memento pour 1928

Ce Calendrier contient

LES TABLEAUX

des

Pierres Précieuses

Porte-Bonheur

As YOU CAN SEE, the notebook is tiny—approximately two by three inches—but its paper is good and thick. Behind the flowered cover, the front flap announces: "This Calendar contains THE CHARTS of Luck-Bearing Precious Stones." The first page advertises the business of a jeweler named Cleper, whose shop is on the boulevard de Strasbourg. The diary is clearly a small favor given to customers or potential customers as a form of advertisement. Louise has it because Cleper worked in her father's shop with her husband, before Cleper split off and opened his own shop. The three men are still friends.

Cleper was very proud of his little diary idea, and gave one to his friend Brunet, who then gave the thing to his wife, as he had no use for something too small to contain his business appointments. The quaint superstition of the copy inside the booklet tickles housewives, which Cleper means to do. Witness the second page:

THE ANCIENTS attributed
Virtues and a Power
of protection to Precious stones

—o—

To ward off ill fortune,
one must wear the
SPECIAL STONE
from the month of one's birth

—o—

To preserve one's health, one must
wear each month a
DIFFERENT STONE

—o—

CONSULT
The Charts of
LUCK-BEARING
PRECIOUS STONES

—o—

CLEPER
JEWELER
PARIS, LA BOURBOULE

The middle spread of the booklet contains a chart of birthstones and what they symbolize, and helpfully points out that such stones can be mounted on rings, barrettes, pendants in platinum, gold, silver. The back page lists which stones must be worn each month to preserve one's health. That Cleper is a clever fellow. His first name is Pierre; clearly, he was born to work with stones, was he not?

The record has not yet yielded a photograph of Pierre Cleper, but this is known: he is a decent-looking man of medium height—not what you would call dashing, but his looks do not explain the fact that he is not married. The fact is that he does not want to marry, ever. He does quite well on his own, thank you very much. He can have a woman when he needs one.

He was in the Great War too, as was every man. Once, the force of the blast from a nearby shell knocked him clean down. Somehow he was uninjured—unsliced by shrapnel, unburned by flame. It was strange. The only thing that happened was that the sound of the explosion made him deaf in his left ear. The other ear works just fine.

P. L. le 3	**Juin**	D.Q. le 11		N.L. le 17	**1928**	P.Q. le 24
1 Ven	Pamp.			16 Sam	Cyr	
2 Sam	Emilie			17 Dim	Avit	
3 Dim	Trinité			18 Lun	Floren	
4 Lun	Emma			19 Mar	G.s. P.	X
5 Mar	Floren.			20 Mer	Sylvèr.	
6 Mer	Claude			21 Jeu	Alice	
7 Jeu	F't.D.			22 Ven	Alban	
8 Ven	Méda⁴			23 Sam	Félix	
9 Sam	Pélag.			24 Dim	Na.s.J.B.	
10 Dim	Landry			25 Lun	Prosp'	
11 Lun	Barna.			26 Mar	Héloïs	
12 Mar	Guy			27 Mer	Adèle	
13 Mer	A.deP.			28 Jeu	Irénée	
14 Jeu	Rufin			29 Ven	Pi. Pa.	
15 Ven	Modes.			30 Sam	Marti.	

Les jours augmentent de 17 minutes.

Louise has not written much in Pierre Cleper's little diary. It floats around on the bottom of her purse, and she digs it out when she needs to scrawl down an address or a telephone number. The only marks she has made on the pages where the months of the year are charted are in June and in July: on the nineteenth day of both these months, she has put a small x, in pencil. To the outside observer, this means nothing.

Les Pierres Précieuses Porte-Bonheur
Spéciales au mois où l'on est né

MOIS	PIERRES	SYMBOLES
JANVIER	Grenat	Loyauté
FÉVRIER	Améthyste	Bonheur, Fortune
MARS	Jaspe sanguin	Courage
AVRIL	Saphir	Vérité, Sagesse
MAI	Émeraude	Espérance, Amour fidèle
JUIN	Agate, Onyx	Prospérité, Longévité
JUILLET	Cornaline, Rubis	Joie, Beauté, Amour
AOUT	Tourmaline	Fermeté
SEPTEMBRE	Chrysolithe, Péridot	Bonté, Bonheur
OCTOBRE	Aigue marine, Opale	Jeunesse, Santé, Amour tendre
NOVEMBRE	Topaze	Amour ardent, Noblesse
DÉCEMBRE	Turqoise	Espérance, Succès

PIERRES FINES MONTÉES SUR BAGUES, Barrettes, Pendentifs en Platine, Or, Argent

Maison fondée **CLEPER** en 1902

Joaillier-Horloger

LA BOURBOULE
Boul. Georges Clemenceau
(face Entrée Grand Établissement)
Téléphone 153

PARIS
30, Boul. de Strasbourg
Téléphone **NORD 39-50**

Did you know, the year of this little memento calendar, 1928?—this is our year. Halfway between the Great War and the Greater War: this is the year of our story. In its waning months, yes—an unusually warm November is when everything begins (Cleper's birthstone chart proclaims November as the month for topaz, the gem of ardent love, nobility). A new family moves into Louise's building, and new things start to happen.

Madame Henri Brunet

THIS IS THE CALLING card for a happy married couple:

M. & Mme HENRI BRUNET

13, rue Thérèse, Paris (1er)

It lists their address—a narrow edifice in the center of Paris, too small to allow for the installation of one of those thrilling creaky elevators that are cropping up in the larger buildings. This is all right by Louise: elevators unnerve her. She does not like the metal grids they are nearly always imprisoned in: an afterthought to the building's design—a violation of the staircase, formerly open. She does not like the jarring clang the grid makes when it shuts after her, when she gets into the small rising box. She is none too fond of the rising box either, encased in its metal shaft: the heave as it pulls her up is a foreign queasy thing, and the closeness makes her nervous, especially if she is in there with another person. It amuses her that they often put a mirror in the elevator, so she can watch the slight shudder of her body as the thing stops abruptly when it reaches the requested floor. Perhaps she can catch the slight widening of her eyes in the reflection, at this moment of vertigo.

Louise likes the building she lives in. It is six stories high with a green front door into a narrow entryway leading to the staircase and a small courtyard in the back. There is a *chambre de bonne* under the roof, a romantic and miserable space where some artist or student always lives. She lives on the third floor. She trudges up and down the stairs several times a day (with and without grocery bags), but she tells herself this keeps her fit. She likes the tile on the landings: stark black and white squares, a chessboard.

This is the calling card for the woman alone:

MADAME HENRI BRUNET

There is no address on this one. What is the meaning of this nearly blank thing, with only the tidy black inscription of a woman's married name? It means that the woman is of comfortable enough means to bother with such an affectation as a calling card.

But what does it signify when her first name is not on the card? What does it mean that all the names that she was born with are not in fact printed on her calling card? This is a funny thing.

If you pay attention, you can see there is something written on the back of the card, pressed hard enough that it makes a slight impression on the front side. Flip the card over—see?

This is her handwriting. This is the handwriting of the owner of the record. If you cannot read it, here is translated what she has written, to remind herself (and you, perhaps):

Mlle. Victor Louise Noémie
Born 13 May 1896
in the 15th Arrondissement

She has underlined her maiden name twice, and underlined it hard—her father's family name. Her Christian name is Louise. She is thirty-two years old.

L'homme illisible

THE ILLEGIBLE MAN IS not in the record; there is no photographic evidence of him. His name is not on any of the documentation. The illegible man does something effete and ineffectual for a living; he makes nothing with his hands. Perhaps he is a professor.

All of the sensuality in his face is in his mouth. There is something lascivious in the full curve of his tremulous lip. This makes sense: he is a man who talks for a living. The spoken word is where he exists most.

Since his youth, his smile has been slightly crooked. As the years have passed, the crookedness has increased. It gives his face something like character. His eyes are light and blank. His hair is dark and receding. He has a florid complexion: the slightest surge of blood is an explosion of red on his cheeks and neck, down into his shirt collar. Because this flush can so easily be seen, he tries not to have too many emotions.

The illegible man is fecund. He has three sons. His wife is pregnant again—he wishes so much for a daughter, this time. His life is continuously saturated in boyness.

The illegible man has beautiful hands with long fingers, with which he gestures eloquently when he lectures. He does not wear a wedding ring, though he owns one. It is a plain yellow gold band, which sits loose in his wife's jewelry box. He does not like the feel of metal against his skin. He does not even wear a wristwatch: he carries a pocket watch. He attaches it to his belt loop with a chain.

He teaches adolescent boys about literature in a school near the Père Lachaise Cemetery. He takes the metro there every day. His last name is Langlais. His first name is not yet known, but he is not far. The illegible man will soon be in the building.

Tu es très gentille, mais pas ce soir

LOUISE HAS ONLY ONE student, these days. Years ago, she was a piano teacher with a sizable roster of pupils; she was making a bit of extra money to save up for the financial burden of all the children she would have with Henri. As the years have gone by, the need for this extra money has decreased: the jewelry shop that Henri runs with Louise's father has grown more prosperous, and also their hope for children has waned. They have been married nine years, and no progeny has arrived. They are not sure what is wrong.

Louise suspects her husband. Louise harbors the conviction that her body is sound; after all, her own mother had two children shortly after marrying her father, in quick succession. She might have had many more, had she not died.

She believes in the fertility of her body, so she thinks Henri must shoot blanks. She will never utter this thought. It is an ugly one for a wife to have.

So, LOUISE STILL HAS the one student, a girl named Garance Saccard, aged fifteen. She comes twice a week, some weeks more. Her parents pay the same fee no matter what, but Louise is happy to give the girl extra lessons: Garance is a talented musician, with a finely calibrated ear. Louise gives her sheet music to take home, gorgeous classical pieces of startling complexity. The girl learns them ridiculously fast and plays them for Louise on the grand piano in her parlor.

Louise's piano is an heirloom, from her mother's family. It is enormous and dark, and takes up half the room. Camille used to love to listen to her play it, back when they were practically children, before the war. Before the war had made them turn to each other as something other than cousins, as a man and a woman. It might not have occurred to them if it weren't for the war, which had changed the urgent yearning for home in his letters into something unexpected. Before he'd written, "Next time I see your face, let me kiss it all over," he'd written, "I wish to be safe at home, running up the stairs at your Papa's house, hearing you call me up on that great big piano."

These days, Louise is too conscious of the way the piano's sound roars across the apartment when it is played; it can be heard in the staircase; it can be heard in the courtyard; it can be heard in the street! This is why Louise can seldom bring herself to play it now: a false note would be an embarrassing thing—nearly public, even though no one could see her flustered face.

Seldom does Garance hit a false note. Louise thinks that she is not teaching the child anything, but the child keeps coming back. The child does not ask for a reference, for the name of a more qualified piano teacher who is more compatible with her soaring virtuosity (an instructor who could get her into the conservatory). The child must love Louise.

When Garance does hit a false note, her cringe is immediate. Her head retracts into her shoulders and she winces sharply, as if someone has slipped a needle into the back of the hand that dared strike the wrong key. Sometimes, Louise can even hear the girl's swift pained inhalation: an error in music—physical discomfort.

Yet the girl does not lift her hands from the keys at such a moment. She plays on through her cringing, fazed for only the smallest hiccup of time. Truly, Louise is privileged to teach this girl. Louise marvels at her luck. After the lesson, she makes tea and they sit in the living room together, sipping it and chatting about this and that and everything. They are friends.

"You know what I like to do, sometimes, at school?" Garance asks, while waiting for her cup to cool enough so that she can pick it up.

"What's that?" Louise is smiling already.

"I like to find the meanest, hardest teacher I have. I like to focus on the one who scares the hell out of all of us students. This year, it's my Math teacher. He's cold and never smiles. When he gets mad, he doesn't yell, but he throws his chalk at us. He's a terror. This man—his name is Dupont—this man Dupont, I go to him after class. After everyone leaves the room as fast as possible to go to lunch, I stay there for a little bit and ask him questions about the magical workings of the quadratic equation. After a while, this makes him soft. After a while, he might even give me a tiny little smile when he passes me in the hallway—but of course not a smile big enough that anyone else can see. Just in his eyes. This is when I know I can begin, you see."

The girl pauses for dramatic effect. Louise swallows her mouthful of tea (too sweet, she has put too much sugar in it) and gazes

44

straight at Garance's liquid green eyes. The girl continues, "After that, when I chat him up, I can talk about other things, like the weather. Maybe what kind of books he likes to read. Maybe he'll even start looking at me like a person, like maybe I'm pretty. One day, he passes me in the hallway, and nods. He nods! He says yes, and I can strike! So, the next time I talk to him, I ask him what his first name is."

"No!"

"Yes! It's wonderful. You should have seen his face. He looked hurt, but he liked it. We had to squirm around each other for a while, but he gave it to me."

Louise titters: "You're not serious! So what's his name?"

"Hubert."

"So this man is your friend now?"

"Ah, no. When I have their full names, I've won. I don't come back."

Louise laughs uproariously, for a long time, until her stomach hurts and tears begin to well in her eyes. Garance laughs with her. It is so good to be alone together, without men, and to discuss such foolish things.

"Garance! You are the naughtiest girl in the world! I don't believe you!"

"You never did things like this when you were a girl?"

"Lord, no! Why would I? Why would you?"

Garance shrugs to indicate her lack of an answer, and the two of them quiver helplessly with mirth in the sun-flooded living room.

———

LOUISE WATCHES HER HUSBAND undress for bed. He loosens his tie and takes it off without unknotting it, as one might slip off a noose, and tosses it onto the dresser.

"You look tired, Henri," she says.

"I am. I had a rough day at work." He unbuttons his shirt with weary slowness, from top to bottom.

"I can help with that," she says, in a soft female exhalation.

"I'm fine."

She thinks maybe he's not getting the picture. So, she puts the book she is reading down on the nightstand without marking the page and flings the covers off her body. She wiggles her nightgown up over the torso and slips it off over her head. She wears nothing underneath. She is completely nude in the yellow light of the bed-side lamp—her skin glows soft and warm. She rolls over onto her stomach and bends one leg up at the knee absentmindedly, like a schoolgirl reading a beauty magazine.

"I can help with that," she repeats.

Her husband beholds her, his shirt now utterly undone but still on him. His hands hang limply at his sides. He sighs, and says: "You're very kind, but not tonight. I'm really very tired."

Suddenly Louise is quite cold. She plucks her nightgown off the floor and puts it back on. She gets back under the covers. She opens her book back up, but is doubly irritated because she cannot recall what page she was on. She flips around the area of the book that looks familiar, trying to remember.

As the rustle of Louise's restless pages fills the silence, Henri finishes taking his clothes off and puts his pajamas on. He slides into bed next to his wife.

"Are you going to be reading for a while?" he asks her.

She does not look over at him as she puts her book away: "No, actually, I think I'm going to sleep now."

"All right, then. Good night, darling."

He reaches across her and flicks off the bedside lamp, leaving her there gazing into the darkness—her startled eyes must take a moment to adjust to this sudden obscurity.

Un jardin public

LOUISE SITS ALONE ON the metro, on her way to church. The one she is going to is nearly a cathedral: it is a great hulking Gothic beast on the edge of the city, not like the baroque candy dish near where she lives. The Baroque candy dish is called Eglise Saint-Roch. She got married there in February of 1919, at the nadir of winter, and has seldom been back inside since.

The wooden slats of the metro seats feel hard against her aching lower back; she is still a bit sore there because of her waning menses. The slight cramping in her lower front will be gone tomorrow, along with the last spots of blood.

The train stops at a station, and Louise sees the lever on the door nearest her swing up as someone yanks it open from the outside. Three men enter the car through the sprung double doors. They are dressed tidily. They settle in the quadrant of seats across the aisle from Louise. She watches them. They are speaking animatedly about some business she does not understand; she can merely feel the abstract flow of money beneath their words. She watches their mouths. Since it is an unseasonably temperate day, the underground is close and warm. The men are wearing wool suits, well cut: brown, gray, and black. The blast of their collective colognes wafts to her—yet the civilized scent of it wilts slightly beneath the heat of their contained bodies: Louise can smell the tang of sweat.

She likes their fashionable high collars, starched to painful stiffness and rounded at the corners. All three of them wear crisp white cotton shirts. She herself is fashionable, with her jaunty violet cloche hat and her long and loose black coat, slipping open at the knees.

The men talk loudly—they gesticulate—they must be excited about something. Something must be at stake. Perhaps they are getting a bit hot under those tight collars of theirs, a little worked up. The one in the black suit takes his jacket off, sliding it off his shoulders without so much as looking at it, and folds it over his arm. He is utterly absorbed in the conversation. Perhaps he is not even entirely aware that he has removed an article of his clothing. Perhaps the heat in his body did not reach the higher parts of his brain before his will responded to it.

Louise looks at the face of the man in the black suit and decides that he is her favorite. He has a handsome jaw: sharply masculine, with a faint hint of scruff, as if his virility is simply too much to be contained by a mere morning shave. His profile is sharp also, with a well-defined nose and a slightly prominent brow ridge. The sound of his voice suddenly bristles with terse authority, and the other two men grow quiet and listen to him for a minute. He continues to speak, as is clearly his right.

Louise is fond of this man, and wonders what his name is. She squirms in her seat, readjusts her position. She rests her hands on her lap, fingers entwined as if in prayer, for after all, she is on her way to church. Today is the last day of October. Tomorrow is the first day of November: All Saints' Day. This is the day on which every good Catholic must visit the graves of their loved ones and clear the weeds around the headstone. Every good Catholic must sweep the family crypt. Every good Catholic must lay fresh flowers at the site where the ones they have lost rot politely and silently into the earth.

Louise will not do this, not even for her mother. After all, she has no memory of the woman; she died when she was born.

IT SMELLS LIKE COLD stone and mildew in the church. Louise genuflects before the altar and crosses herself with the holy water: "In the name of the Father and of the Son and of the Holy Spirit—amen." She takes off her wedding ring and places it on her right hand. She is lucky today: there is no one ahead of her in line. She goes into the confession booth without having to wait.

It is dim inside the booth, and wood creaks as she kneels.

"Bless me, Father, for I have sinned. It has been a week since my last confession."

It has been a bit longer than that, but this is a small lie.

"I am listening, my child."

The gravelly, disembodied voice behind the grid startles her as if she hadn't expected it. She closes her eyes, clears her throat, and begins: "Last night I consummated a sexual union with a man to whom I am not married."

She pauses for emphasis. The labored wording she exchanges with the priest during these times is part of what makes the entire ritual so compelling: it is part of what makes her smile to herself in the shadows. She continues.

"His name was Jean-François. I don't even know his last name: we met only yesterday in a public garden. He was so handsome, with a rough sandpaper chin and a jaw you could cut things with. His voice utterly hypnotized me—I was a helpless girl, Father. He took me to his apartment immediately. He told me I was beautiful— and repeated it! He did everything with such ease and charm— oh, Father, he must do this with a new woman every day! I surrendered so completely that I nearly fell asleep in his arms—but then he undressed me, so quickly that I did not know what happened! I didn't say no. It felt too good. He told me that I was a gorgeous thing, but that I must not fall in love. I laughed then, when he presumed to forbid me such foolishness! Do you know, Father, I began to come the moment he penetrated me? Oh—the entire time it was so warm and slippery—such a long time—he did not make a sound, except right at the end when he ejaculated—he groaned then, and I thought I would faint from the pleasure of it, Father, though I knew exactly how wrong it was! I don't know: is such a thing forgivable?"

There is an uncomfortable lag on the other side of the screen. For several seconds, the priest doesn't speak. Louise fancies that she can hear his robe rustling as he shifts in utter bewilderment. Finally, the blessed male voice manifests again:

"Ah . . . well, ah . . . every sin is forgivable, my child, if you have faith."

Louise has to put both hands up to her mouth to smother her imminent laughter. Her inner snickering is so loud that she does not even hear the penance that is dispensed to her. The penance is a useless thing; it is not what she comes for.

When she steps out of the dank church into the bright daylight, she takes her wedding ring off her right hand and puts it back in its proper place.

This—this false confession—this is one of Louise's favorite hobbies.

TODAY IS FRIDAY, THE second day of November. Though most shops are closed because everyone is taking the long weekend for the All Saints' holiday, Henri is not home but at work. This is not so bad, because Garance is over at Louise's. They do not sit in the living room and sip tea, however, because this afternoon is too exciting for that. A new family is moving into the building. The massive truck filled with all their worldly possessions blocks the narrow little street below entirely. Garance and Louise are at the window together, leaning against the ledge and looking down at this truck, at all the happenings surrounding it.

The movers heave furniture down the ramp into the street with great difficulty. They negotiate carrying it up the curb and into the front door of the building. Every step is a heavy challenge and must be performed slowly, with discomfort. Louise would amuse herself by picturing the labor in the straining musculature of the movers, except she is too interested in the new family. She keeps catching unsatisfactorily short glances of them as they dash back and forth in a flutter of excitement and anxiety, hoping that nothing gets broken as they are installed into their new home.

There are several children, all boys with smooth blond hair, as far as Louise can see. There seem to be dozens of them, but she has not seen more than two together at any given moment. Surely, there must be more than two?

"They must have paid extra to get those guys out here on a holiday," Garance observes of the movers, who are red-faced with their efforts.

"They must have. It's a good idea for the family, though, to have a couple of days to settle in before going back to school and work."

They are quiet again as they watch. Louise looks at the woman of the house, who is explaining something about the exquisite delicacy and monetary worth of her glass-topped reading lamps to one of the movers, who looks glazed and bored. The woman is mildly plump but pretty, with the same straight blond hair as her boys and a round face with delicate features. She wears loose billowy clothes that obscure the shape of her body, but Louise swears that she sees a slight swelling in the drapery sheathing her abdomen. Louise thinks the woman must be pregnant—yes, the woman is pregnant and this pains Louise, though she has never met this person before. This pains her because she is so jealous of the woman and of her fine sons, her little boys who run circles around her, shouting with glee and excitement—this woman, her fine sons, and yet more incipient life ripening in her body!

And she, Louise—an empty vessel. Truly, for no good reason, the sight of this woman she has never met before pains her.

"Louise." Garance elbows her teacher in the side. "Louise, that man is so handsome, he shouldn't be allowed!"

"Allowed to what?" Louise asks without averting her gaze from the woman, though she knows what Garance means. Always, she is willfully obtuse with the girl, in order to squeeze the words out of her.

"Allowed to walk around!" the girl squeals.

Louise turns her head to look at this marvel of a man that Garance is gawking at, and at this moment the same man looks up straight into her face, his attention grabbed by Garance's lusty yelp.

From the third floor, Louise cannot tell what color his eyes are, but she can tell that he has a startlingly beautiful mouth, ripe with pinkness. The proportions of his lithe body are Greek in perfection. Her gaze is attracted even by his bare forearms; he has rolled up his shirtsleeves to the elbows. Truly, she cannot see a damn thing wrong with his looks. He must be the woman's husband. He must be the head of the house. He gives Louise a brief tight smile and a small nod in greeting, and does not wait for a greeting to be returned before he goes back to his business of directing the movers.

"Good Lord," Louise says softly, "you're right. His face alone is a war crime against all women."

The girl is cringing in embarrassment, attempting to shrink her body as if to hide. She whispers: "Do you think he heard what I said?"

"He heard your voice, since he looked up, but from down there, I'm sure he couldn't make out your words."

"You think so?"

"I know it."

This assertion seems to calm the girl, and the two of them return to their gazing. They agree, after a few more minutes, that there are in fact three distinct boys in this new family, but not more. There are no girls to be seen.

A car pulls into the narrow one-way street, right behind the moving truck and the furniture that is constantly being poured out of the back of it. The car can decidedly not go forward; its path is irredeemably blocked. The lone man inside is upset by this, and gives a succinct honk. When he gets no response, he leans on his horn. Two of the movers come around to take a look at him. Yelling ensues, with colorful language. Louise and Garance are entertained by this new development. The impotent displays of male fury go on unabated for a good half minute, until the man of the house comes around the side of the truck himself, and stands in front of all of them, with his arms crossed over his chest.

"Are you the boss?" the fellow in the car demands.

"In a manner of speaking," the man says.

"You have to get this bloody mess out of the street!"

"Not for a while. I would appreciate if all of you would refrain from using such language in front of my sons, please."

The man's simple civility disarms all of them. They are quiet.

"But I must get through," the fellow in the car says rather plaintively.

"Well, you cannot, and such is the state of things. You will have to back up, and find another way around; it can't be that complicated. Or are you such a shoddy pilot that you do not know how to engage your machine into reverse?"

The man enunciates clearly enough that Louise and Garance can hear his every word, though he does not raise his voice. His tone is not angry: it is merely a statement of what must be, with an edge of mocking dismissal rising into the last question. His voice admits no objection—Louise thinks its authority is even more attractive than that of the black-suited man on the metro. She is dizzy with admiration.

The fellow and his car back away swiftly and disappear with a great grinding of gears.

"Oh, that was magnificent!" Garance laughs as the furniture-hauling in the street down below resumes. "Louise, I think I've fallen in love, haven't you?"

LATER, LOUISE HAS TO run an errand. On the way out of the building, she stops by the mailboxes, on the off chance that the new family has already bothered putting their name up by their slot. She thinks that this is unlikely, but is pleasantly surprised. The name is already there, on a tiny metal placard. The type is white on navy blue, in all capitals.

LANGLAIS

the type spells.

The placard is clearly something they had wrought for this very purpose. It is a well crafted and charming object. Louise thinks it a bit terse, for her own placard reads:

M. & Mme Henri Brunet

There is no monsieur on the Langlais sign, nor a madame. But perhaps this is reflective of the nature of the head of the house: he does not indulge in unnecessary words. Every letter must count. Still, Louise is disappointed that his first name is not displayed. To learn it, she will just have to wait until she is properly introduced.

Paris

February 10th

Dear Sir,

Something has been going around among the people I work with—just when the sickness was dying down and I thought I was safe, it came for me. Also, it has been dreadfully cold lately in Paris: it has hovered around −10°C for a while now, which, like the snow I told you about earlier, is a highly unusual occurrence for this part of the world. Had I imagined such frigid temperatures were a possibility, I would have brought one of my funny-looking down-filled monster coats from my years in Michigan. I did not, however, and brought with me a very smart-seeming black wool coat that makes me look quite dashing but is absolutely useless to me in this absurd weather: I was destroyed by my desire for fashion.

In any case, my entire musculature is seized with pointless hurt, and I feel awful. My head is stuffed with mucus-logged cotton and I am in a constant vomitous haze. I violently regurgitate anything solid. I called the secretary this morning to let her know I was not coming in, and she actually came over to my apartment to make me soup! It was certainly unexpected. I did not even know she was in the least fond of me: she has behaved quite crisply toward me, as I am one of many foreign professors she must push paper around for. Such are the French: I cannot even tell when they care for me.

She busied herself in my kitchen for a while, and then brought me the soup on a tray. She sat at the foot of my bed and watched me sip it gingerly like the grateful invalid that I am.

57

"Vous avez besoin de quelque chose d'autre?"[3] she asked after a bit.

I shook my head no, as my throat is so scruffed that speaking pains me. She surprised me then by looking upon me with something like motherly tenderness and saying:

"Pauvre Trevor, vous avez attrapé une grosse crève."[4]

I laughed then, though it was uncomfortable. It was the first time she called me anything besides Monsieur Stratton, though she still addressed me in the formal second person.

In any case, in my weakened state, I was flooded with irrational love for my secretary and her unexpected kindness toward me—her name is Josianne, by the way. I nearly died some sort of little brain death and told her about the record when she asked me how my research was going. This record—I could get in some degree of hot water for not sending it to Preservation, and I nearly told a coworker about it! She looked at me somewhat piercingly when I told her my work was coming along just fine, as if she were evaluating me, as if she knew there was something I very much wanted to tell her and then didn't. I must have imagined that strange flicker of intensity in those striking hazel eyes. Most likely, she does not care a great deal about the research business of us fusty academics, and what we may consider correct in that regard.

And yet what a moment! It is entirely probable that had my body not been such a vanquished wreck of illness, I might have felt the impulse to make love to her. The woman was, after all, sitting on my

---

3. "Do you need anything else?"
4. "Poor Trevor, you caught a damn big cold."

bed. Truly, sometimes the French have a bizarre effect upon me.

Ah, I'm sorry, Sir: I tell you too much! Chalk it up to my having a variety of drowsy medicines in my bloodstream at the moment, and also to the queer fact that my body seems to forget how miserable it is when I am writing, these days. I study the record in an attempt to help my fever, so without further meandering, my latest findings:

1. a letter from "Victor, Camille—Sous-officier" to "Mademoiselle Louise Victor," dated 31 October 1915.
2. a letter from the front lines in Belgium, from Camille Victor to his cousin, whom he affectionately calls Louisette—dated 28 June 1915.
3. a strange and lovely object that is something like a postcard, and something like a greeting card: a marriage of paper and lace that I find odd and cannot completely understand—dated 22 November 1915 (also from Camille to his Louisette—something strange happened when I translated this one).
4. a postcard on which the date and location are not indicated, from Camille to Louise once again.
5. two bullet cartridges fused end to end to make a pencil case. The thing is almost the length of my entire hand, painstakingly engraved.

I must say, this particular excursion into Louise Brunet took a bit out of me. If I have to translate another word about exploding bullet wounds and romantic longing, I will never stop throwing up.

As I take my leave, allow me to indulge in a nibble of tortured

Gallic courtesy. It manifests itself most vividly in their business correspondence. The French have at their disposal a veritable arsenal of groveling closing salutations. Their ornate obsequiousness borders on the obscene. They are so succulent on the page that the tastiness of our terse American "Sincerely" fades on the tongue by comparison. Thus, allow me to offer you such a salutation presently:

Je vous prie d'accepter, Cher Monsieur, l'expression de mes sentiments les plus distingués,[5]

Trevor Stratton

Trevor Stratton

PS—Look, I have made myself a calling card on my word processor. Sometimes computers can be of amusement. Witness:

MONSIEUR TREVOR NEVILLE STRATTON

Nulle Part (aidez-moi!)

---

5. *I pray that you will accept, Dear Sir, the expression of my most distinguished sentiments*

[NB: If I were to jot my true name and location on the back of the card for you, as Louise has done with her calling card—if I were to translate for you, though you can doubtlessly understand the simple vocabulary I employ here, the scrawl would read:

Mister Trevor Neville Stratton

No Where (help me!)

I will sleep now.]

[NB: Here is a scan of the outside of the envelope. Look at how careful and slow is the work of his nib. Look at the curlicues he has so patiently drawn under the girl's name, and how straight his underlines, as if done with a ruler. On this envelope, the date of the letter inside has been quickly scrawled in pencil, presumably by the owner of the record—perhaps she liked to keep things in order—in which case, who has scrambled everything?]

[NB: I have looked on a map for this town Louise lived in, named Malakoff, which is a slightly unusual name for a French place. It is not far from Paris, off the river Seine. The ink on all this correspondence is a warm brown, but I suspect it was initially black and has faded. In places, you can still see where Camille's nib fades off a little and he has to dip it again. The paper is thick and good; it has stood the test of time.]

At the Army, on 31-10-15

My Little[6] Louisette

Thank you for your sweet little package: it gave me great pleasure. I hasten to write you to let you know how I'm getting on, and to thank you. The news is still good apart from some aches I have in my legs; this pain is a recurrence from

---

6. It must be indicative of some national trait I do not thoroughly understand that the word *petit/petite* is so often a tender endearment to the French. People who love each other call each other Little This and Little That. I might find it a bit demeaning, but they seem to revel in it. They seem to enjoy being Little Things that can be held and cradled, warmly.

last winter and must mean that the new winter is coming in. I have received a letter from your little Father two nights ago, and I replied right away [. . .].[7] I will tell you that your package's arrival was a surprise for me. I was lying down and dozing off when I heard someone call Sergeant Victor, so I was awakened with a start and I thought that it was my sister's package which I expected, but look at that! It didn't look like the thing I expected: it turned out to be you, Dear Louisette, who didn't forget me—except you had forgotten the exact address, and I was lucky to receive it. I am including with this letter the address that you put down: you will laugh when you see it. As I could not have a ring made for you since I am no longer in the trenches,[8] I will send you tomorrow a little package containing 1 penholder made with 2 fused German cartridges, and engraved. One side is for the pencil, and the other for the nib. I hope, My Louisette, that you will keep it as a souvenir. Not much to tell you other than good health and no bad blood. Say hello to our Aunt for me.

    I embrace you well and hard

          from afar

  Your cousin who thinks of you

      and who loves you

        Camille

---

7. [meaning lost]

8. What did they make these rings out of in the trenches? I wonder.

[NB: My translation is difficult. I do not know if I am staying true to the original; it is difficult to render his muddled voice while remaining intelligible. Likely, when I turn the record in to Preservation, the letters will be looked at and catalogued by more qualified scholars than myself—more adept at translation and history. I cannot identify the uniforms in the photos; I do not understand the references to many places and dates: really, I know nothing. Yet I cannot stop the compulsion burning in my hands and in my heart to piece it together myself, as if I have been chosen to do so. Oh, and here is scanned Louise's wrong address, included with the letter—

]

[NB: I picked up this letter because it is not addressed in gorgeous intricate ink like the others. It is addressed in pencil, and quite ragged. See the envelope?

The enclosed letter is on lined pages. As you might be able to see, the letter was first written in pencil. Then the boy went over his pencil with the nib. However, he did not have time to let the ink dry properly, did not have time to erase the pencil. This makes the entire letter look blurry, like panicked vision, rendering it difficult to read. Oh—Camille did not have time to sign in ink over his own name, and he did not have time to write in ink over his location information. He did not have time to address the envelope as prettily as he usually does. What was happening to him? Who was ordering him where? His name at the end of the missive, in mere pencil—

        his name: a thing that can be erased.]

14 Heures 30

- Belgique, le 28 juin 1915.

Ma Petite Cousine.

Je viens de recevoir ta petite lettre du 26 juin qui m'as fait un grand plaisir. je continue à aller bien pour le moment apart comme je te disais un petit mal de tête assez constant, enfin je finis par m'y habituer. j'ai pu comme tu me dis Chère Louisette me reposer et trouver cela un peu meilleur que les tranchées. je suis à ma compagnie et je serais comme tu me le demandes bon avec les hommes apart des fois ou il y a une exception car la plupart des hommes qui se trouvent aux Bataillons sont tous des apaches et des voleurs. et des fois nous sommes obligés car étant gradé de punir brutalement. et il y en a qui attrape 10 ans de prison a faire après la Campagne contre les Austro-allemands,

Tu vois Ma Louisette que notre vie n'est pas rose et que ce n'est pas le métier rêver aux Bataillons. Je suis peiné aussi beaucoup d'apprendre que ton petit père se rapproche de la ligne meurtrière car je lui souhaite d'aller au feu la plutard qu'il le pourrai.

Car Ma Chère Louisette tu ne peut pas te figurer
la boucherie humaine quia créer cette guerre effroyable
il faut y aller pour le croire et nous sommes obligés de
ne rien raconté car sans cela on est punis.
J'ai vu plusieurs fois des hommes et mêmes de mes
amis sauté en l'air par un obus qui avait
éclaté et après quil avait éclaté on retrouvais un
homme en une dizaine de morceaux. Ou bien
ce sont les balles explosives qui à l'entrée font
un trou gros comme un crayon et à la sortie
de la plaie est plus grand que le creux de la
main. Alors tu dois penser si cela fais souffrir.
J'ai vu aussi au début que je suis arrivé aux
environs d'Arras en fin Janvier car voici bientot
6 mois que je suis à la guerre un obus de
220 m. à tombée sur une section de 60 hommes
rassemblés et prête à partir aux tranchées et bien
après l'explosion 52 hommes étaient étendus à terre
ce qui te prouve la boucherie et la cruauté
de cette guerre.
C'est terrible ma Pauvre Louisette et tout le monde
commence à en avoir assez et voudrais bien

68

voir la fin prochaine, mais c'est toujours
avec un calme et un courage inouï que
nous nous battons et nous chantons en mon-
tant aux tranchées pour oublier souffrance
et misère. Mais je crois ma Petite Louisette
que cet hiver qui vient verra encore la guerre
et c'est pénible d'y penser surtout de
repasser les nuits de Novembre Décembre et
Janvier sous la pluie, la gelée, et la neige —
comme nous les avons déjà passer et d'attrap-
per les pieds gelés ou les douleurs et les rhu-
matismes que la guerre nous donne à
volonté. Enfin on a toujours le moral bon
et l'idée de tous vous revoir un jour
en criant « Vive la France ».
Je suis content que mon Oncle Eugène aille
mieux car d'être malade aliter ce n'est
pas amusant. et je lui souhaite de se réta-
blir vivement, Au sujet de Gégène tu le
remercieras de m'avoir fait souhaiter le
bonjour mais tu lui diras qu'il me donne
son adresse cela tu dois le penser me
feras un grand plaisir.

Je n'est pas encor eut connaissacce avec
la lettre de la Cousine comme tu dis
Car si il y a longtemps que ma Tante
Marine ma écris sa lettre c'est peut-être
perdue ou peut-être retournée pendant que
j'étais à l'ambulance 2/46. Je ne vois
plus grand chose à te dire que de
souhaiter le bonjour à ma Tante Marie

Je t'embrasse bien fort des tranchées

Ton Cousin qui t'aime et qui
pense à toi —

Camille

Sergent : au
3ᵉ Bataillon de Marche
2ᵉ Compagnie
1ᵉ Section
Secteur postal. 68.

14:30

Belgium, on 28 June 1915

My Little Cousin,

I just received your letter from 26 June, which gave me great pleasure. I'm still all right for the moment apart from, as I've told you before, a little headache that is rather constant— well, eventually I got used to it. I was able to rest as you've told me to, Dear Louisette, and have found this a bit better than the trenches. I am with my company, and I will be good to the other men, as you ask of me—except in cases when they fail me, as most of the men who find themselves in the Battalions are all apaches and thieves. Sometimes, we the ranked men have to brutally punish them and some have caught 10-year prison terms after the Campaign against the Austro-Germans.

You see, My Louisette, that our life is not a bed of roses and that being at the Battalions is not a dream job. I am also pained to learn that your little father is approaching the front lines I hope that he reaches the front as late as possible.

Because My Dear Louisette, you cannot figure the human butchery of this horrifying war. You have to be there to believe it and we are not allowed to tell of it: otherwise they punish us.

Several times, I have seen men (and even my friends) blown up into the air by shells landing—and after the detonation you can find a man in a dozen pieces. Or, there are exploding bullets which make a hole no wider than a pencil at the point of entry, but the exit wound is bigger than the palm of the hand. You can imagine that this makes us suffer.

In the beginning, when I arrived around Arcus near the end of January—it's been nearly six months since I've been at war—a 220-mm shell fell on a 60-man section, all of them gathered and ready to leave for the trenches. After the explosion, 52 men were fallen, on the ground, which proves the butchery and the cruelty of this war.

It's terrible, my Poor Louisette, and everyone is beginning to have enough and would like to see the end of this. Still, we keep fighting with such unbelievable courage and calm and we sing in the trenches to forget suffering and misery. But it is my belief, my Little Louisette, that this coming winter will see more war and it is difficult to think of it—especially spending nights again in November and December in the rain, the frost, the snow. As we have already spent a winter in this state, we know the frozen feet and the pains and the rheumatisms that this war gladly dispenses. In the end, morale is good and we still harbor the belief that we will all see each other one day, shouting, "Vive la France."

I am glad that Uncle Eugène is feeling better because being ill is no fun—I wish him a swift recovery. Speaking of Gégène, do thank him for sending his greetings and let him know that if he wishes to send me his address (you must know this) it will give me great pleasure.

I haven't received our cousin's letter—and it has been a long time since Aunt Marie has written me. Perhaps her letter was lost, or maybe it was returned while I was at the 2/45 ambulance. I don't know what else to tell you other than to send my greetings to Aunt Marie.

I embrace you well and hard from the trenches.

Your cousin who loves you and who
thinks of you—

Camille

Sergeant: in the
3rd Infantry Battalion
2nd Company
1st Section
Postal Sector 68

[NB: Now, I wish that I had not picked up this ragged envelope, for translating this has doubtlessly given fuel to my fever images—this tremendous rush of movement and color that seizes me by the throat when the temperature in my body spikes. Now if I listen I can almost hear the echo of a gunshot, and what is this? A delicate pretty thing. A postcard. Look at the detailed embossing around its perimeter and the embroidery. Are the colors not vivid? The embroidery adorns a fine gossamer mesh pouch, with a fine gossamer flesh map—oh goodness, I mean a fine gossamer mesh flap. Inside this pouch is slipped a tiny card—a card within a card. What an idea, to give such respects to a simple postcard. These days, we do not bestow such flowery love upon mere paper.]

[NB: The following is the text on the back of the card, which I realize now was written the very same day as the marriage proposal letter I sent you with my first packet. Here, too, he has drawn pencil lines to make sure that his words go straight across. He must think this is an important letter. He must respect the lovely paper on which he bestows his sentiment.]

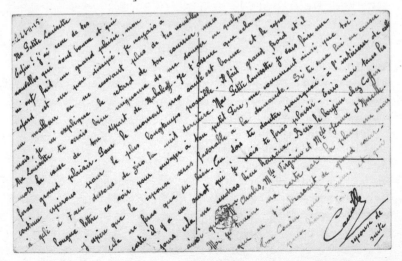

On 22-11-15

My Little Louisette

Finally! I have received news of you. That this news is good gives me great pleasure: my depression[9] has dissipated a little. I thought something ill had happened when I didn't receive any word from you, but I've come to terms with the lateness of your mail. But, My Louisette, you would be very sweet to tell me a few words on the reason for your departure from Malakoff. I assure you that this would please me. For the moment, my health is good, and I've been granted some rest (let us hope for as long as possible). It is very cold and it froze to 7 below zero last night. My Little Louisette, I'm going to write a long letter to your little Father, concerning me as well as you. I hope that the response will be favorable to the request.[10] If you'd

---

9. One of the French words for depression is *cafard,* which the boy employs here, and which I find noteworthy. Another meaning of this word is "cockroach." So when a Frenchman says "J'ai le cafard," he means he is depressed and he is also literally saying "I have the cockroach," as if some vile hard-shelled scuttling insect vermin is crawling all over his brain—how dreadful. It's a bit vivid for me, I'm afraid.

10. Louise's father did not like this request. At first he was merely angry: he stalked around the house grumbling at the idea of his daughter marrying the half-wit child of his half-wit brother. Not a good boy, to be sure—he'd had a phase as a schoolyard bully that had unsettled the family. There was a lot of talk about the army straightening him out, but how could one be sure? There was no way to know.

He turned to look at his daughter then, saw all the worried hope in her expectant face. Clearly she had in mind that he would rant his way out of the initial shock and eventually acquiesce. He went dark at that moment, more terrible than she'd ever seen him. The cold words that came from him stunned her with pain: "You will not marry your own blood, and that is all. The war might be turning us into animals, but we must have our limits. You have pained me deeply by entertaining such relations with your own cousin. You will stop this. Here is the letter he sent me. You will destroy it."

like to discuss it with him, this would only do good. You must suspect why—inside this card is a secret I believe will give you pleasure. If you write me every day, this shall make me very happy. A warm hello to Coffin and also Mme Charles, Mlle Virginie and Mlle Jeanne, and Marcelle. I must finish my card for I am running out of room—I embrace you full-heartedly. Your Cousin who loves you and thinks of you—Camille

  Reply to follow

[NB: The following is the card within the card—the *secret,* as the boy calls it. Despite his horrid spelling and his atrocious punctuation, you can see Camille is clever: he has punned. If you look very closely at the front side of the card, you can just make out that he has rubbed off the manufactured greeting that was previously there and written in his own hand, "Thoughts of the absent." The French word for "thought" (*pensée*) is also the French word for "pansy," which is the flower pictured therein. So, he is giving her flower/thoughts, on paper:

 She did not understand until much later why the idea of her marrying her own blood infuriated him so. Marriage between cousins was, after all, not so uncommon.

 [NB: How do I have this information? It is not in any of the documentation.]

To my sweet Louisette

> Thoughts towards the absent
> Are the prettiest things
> For those that spill their blood
> Under a mournful gaze
> What happiness upon return
> For two hearts filled with love
> For Victory smiles
> To our Love dear.
>
> Camille Victor
> On 26-11-15

77

As you can see, the poem on the minuscule card is dated four days after the note on the larger card. Did the boy carry the message on him the whole time? On his body, tucked into his jacket next to his frenetic heart? Do you think he kept it so long because he was frightened? More frightened of her reply and of the reply of her father than of being blown to bits by the enemy? But he sent it off—he sent it, the dear boy—the fever is on me, oh my line breaks—

I can feel them, their pure animal terror as they await the next explosion—
this ill black mire they fight in—can you smell it?
Can you smell the fluids from all the bodies
of the fallen

      seeping into this mud

          as they decompose:

               human rot corrupting the very earth.
And this poor makeshift hospital unclean and filled with the groans of our pointless suffering. In this place, we run out of even the doubtful succor of morphia's oblivion. Do you know they hack at our bones?

      Through our flesh, when the limb cannot be saved—

               the doctors saw it off.

We are shells and we are shrapnel—we are the surprise detonation arcing in from the sky, showering all in slicing bits of metal and fire. We are howls of bewildered agony as we crumple to the ground—blown open—bits of our gore everywhere—

               our blood seeping.
This is if we are lucky: if there are recognizable parts of us that can be found. Sometimes, when the thing comes right for us—right on

top of us—it turns us into Nothing—we cannot be foraged, not even a single chunk of our obliterated meat.

(Such attrition would make even victory a pallid thing.)

Our shell shock and our thousand-yard stare—we are stunned into quiet by the images that cannot be erased and thus erase all else—our gaze so still and so quiet that it can be ignored, if you wish, you do not have to

listen to our silence.

Digging this trench so hard, the muscle fibers in our backs bursting with the hurt of this: our last ditch effort.

Our shell shock and our thousand-yard stare—

I gaze ever farther than that.

For miles and miles I stare, through everything and straight to you. As I fight, I keep my eyes always on you: I cannot bear the stricken look on your face should you be told that I have died—

your face—

it is the only reason I am still alive.]

Un Souvenir

❦

A POSTCARD:

11

Look at what the ornate white type says, at the corner of the postcard: "Un Souvenir." A memory.[12]

This is a funny thing in our time: the thought of sending a postcard home depicting ourselves in the battlefield being attacked,

---

11. Look at these two, all buttoned up. Look at the one in the trench, below the shoddy woodwork and the crumpled tarp. He looks up at the lens wearily. He does not bother to remove his pipe from his mouth for the photo. He stirs some hot, comforting beverage with a large spoon. There is a picture of his beloved wife propped up at his elbow. All you can tell is that she looks quite illuminated, with a large hat. At the moment, the husband doesn't look at his wife but at you. He wonders what you're doing here.

The other one, the one standing, stares dreamily into the distance, with both hands in his pockets to shield them from the frigid air. Aren't you impressed at how tidy he keeps his mustache, under the circumstances? Wait—is that a sword dangling at his side? They still fought with swords?

This must be wrong. Not in the twentieth century!

But this is not wrong—did you know, in the beginning, there were still cavalry charges? It was ridiculous. There were so many pointless deaths this way, of both men and horses.

His bayonet is taller than he is; it must be a heavy burden to carry around everywhere. The blade is a long sharp cruel thing: it can run a man straight through, right through the sternum and into the heart—it slides in so easily. The lack of resistance from the flesh and bone of the enemy startles him every time.

The blade is long and sharp and cruel and carefully maintained. It must also be carefully wielded: he wouldn't want to accidentally gut himself. That would be quite a foolish way to die, by your own clumsy hand.

12. Do you see in the background? There is rendered a shell explosion, with the flaming shrapnel radiating outward, painted red to differentiate it from the smoke. Imagine the sound of this blast. The two men do not even bother turning their heads to look at where the racket comes from. Are they that blasé, or is the picture a completely posed and manufactured thing?

Whether they are truly at the trenches, or whether this was cleverly done in a studio somewhere, you know that the explosion at the horizon behind the two men is painted in by an artist's hand—it is not really there.

cringing for cover, with our weapons and our packs close to our bodies—postcards are a thing to send home from a vacation, are they not?

Still, look at this postcard. It declares unabashedly that it is a memory, and it is right, for butchery is often what memories are made of. Since you have it in your hand, why not flip it over and find out whom it is from?

It reads, simply:

> A thousand kisses,
> Camille

It is addressed, of course, to his beloved Louise. It was dashed off quickly because, as you can perhaps see, the boy's signature bleeds a little, the curve of the C and the dot in the i especially. It is unlike him to be so careless with his writing implements; he must have been on his way somewhere. He had time to send only the fastest thought, the one thing he truly needed to dispense to Louise before shooting off to a dangerous place: a thousand kisses.

There is another object—(No, please! Save us! Have pity on us! Not another of those painful souvenirs! Spare us the searing burn of another memory!)

This is the last one for a little while, I promise. Besides, you really should see it. It is an interesting artifact.

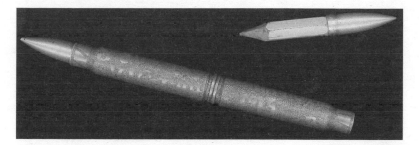

You see? This is the present that Camille sent to Louise the day after his letter dated 31 October 1915: "a little package containing 1 penholder made with 2 fused German cartridges, and engraved." Look, the pencil is still inside, after all this time.

The two bullet shells are welded together, butt to butt, to make a sort of useful thing, an object made to amuse instead of kill. Isn't it sweet, to make captured weaponry into a memory, into a writing implement? You could pick up this killing metal and write a story with it. Look at the engraving along the metal shaft. It reads:

VICTOR

CAMILLE—

SOUVENIR

on one side, and on the other

1914
CAMPAGNE
1915
DE L'YSER

Go on, you can put the tip of the bullet back in and pick up the object to take a better look at it, like so:

Its coolness rolls easily along the palm of your upturned hand. It feels chilly and ticklish, downright pleasant. Now, grasp these two fused German cartridges and press the bullet tip into the pad of your thumb. Go ahead: it doesn't hurt. It's just a little bit of pointed pressure. It's a bit sharp, though, isn't it?

Take the object and aim it right between your eyes. Strike yourself with it lightly. That dull thunk padded by a thin layer of your flesh, that's your skull. Imagine if that bullet you're holding were traveling very fast—if it were traveling its destined speed out the dark mouth of some heated gun—and struck you in the head. The sharp point would penetrate into the bone with disconcerting ease. Your cranial plate might shatter from the impact, a little. That huge bullet (about the size of your middle finger) would get lodged good and tight in your brain.

Wait—there's more.

You could hold it up to the side of your trachea and press there.

Your breath might come a little more labored. Imagine the bullet ripping through your throat at this place: the air sucked clean out of you in the most painful second of your life.

Usually though, you don't see it coming. Often, you get shot in the back. It could hit you right at the base of the spine, a little to the right—just where the padded flesh of your buttock tapers to an end. It will shred its way through the springy muscle tissue at your waistline, then tear its way through your viscera like so much tissue paper. The bullet will fall not far from your feet, slickly covered in your blood, but you won't see it. You will be too busy being aghast at the gaping hole in your gut, from which your entrails will begin to spill. It will hurt so much that you will have no idea what to do with yourself except scream like you have never screamed before.

You will fall to your knees, pressing down on your gushing wound with the flats of both helpless hands. Your blood spurting from your innards—all over your clothes—in your agony you will topple. What will you do next?

I CAN SEE THAT you are getting a bit nervous now. I can see that I am becoming confused between what is me and what is you and what is them. For the moment (now that you have the smell of warmed-up metal embedded in the palms of your sweaty hands), you may put the object back down and recede from this unpleasant thought.

Il faut de la peau

IT IS MONDAY, NOVEMBER 5, 1928, the start of the week after All Saints' Day. Louise has spent a pleasant weekend with her husband. He even made love to her. This was good.

Nevertheless, Henri is back at work at the moment (it is four in the afternoon), so she is alone in the apartment again. Garance is not coming over today, and Louise does not have any immediate errands to run, so she feels restless. Of course, she could always clean something. However, this prospect does not excite her. Instead, she dashes a note on the first page of the small notepad of disposable mulch paper on which she writes her grocery lists:

Dear Sir,
—in either case not a good idea—adultery?

The whole swirling delight of it—such mutual possession is what we all live for, is it not?

Can you commit adultery without any skin-on-skin contact? No no. That is absurd. There must be skin.

Please agree to the expression of my most
distinguished sentiments,

Madam

She looks, stunned, at what she has just written. She tears the paper off the top of the notepad. She has not pressed hard on the pencil, so the imprint of what she has just put forth is not on the next page. The moment was a soft one, cleanly contained on the sheet for which it was meant.

Louise considers crumpling the paper and throwing it away. She decides not to, for the wording of her message amuses her. It diverts her that she does not even know the full name of this Sir, and thus cannot presume to address him with it. Her closing salutation also pleases her: a thing meant for business correspondence. She asks herself: what manner of business is this?

She decides to slide this peculiar eruption of hers into an envelope that she digs out from her husband's desk. She slowly licks the flap and seals it with the pad of her thumb, right there on the smooth lacquered surface where Henri writes his company checks. She looks around the room, sits down. She realizes that she is still holding her grocery-list pencil, but she decides that this will not do. She addresses the envelope with her husband's fountain pen, writing slowly and smoothly, like when she was a girl at school who paid great attention to her penmanship because she was evaluated on it as much as on content.

Monsieur Langlais,

she writes, and then writes his address, the same as her address.

If she truly wants to send him this, it would be very easy: she could drop it directly in his mailbox the next time she leaves the building. A casual sideways gesture, as if to steady herself for a moment—a loosening of the fingers, and the missive will drop soundlessly into the slot, where only the man himself will be able to get it back, with his mail key.

He, or his wife!

It is addressed to him, though, and surely she does not presume to open his correspondence?

She looks for a stamp among her husband's things and finds a book of them. She tears one off, sticks it on the envelope, and goes to the post office around the corner immediately. Though the post is efficient, the sun is already sliding down and dimming, so the letter will certainly not be delivered until tomorrow. Then the scrawled note will be slipped back into the same building it came out of. Why does Louise bother to cancel a stamp, to make herself wait longer? She is strange that way.

It doesn't matter. She is almost entirely certain nothing will come of this. When she sends off the envelope, her hand doesn't hesitate. Her heart doesn't even skip a beat. Afterward, she buys herself a *pain au chocolat* at the nearest bakery and goes for a leisurely stroll in the nearest public garden, the one called Palais Royal.

LOUISE IS AT THE center of the garden, at the large round stone fountain. She is sitting on one of the metal chairs left there by the City of Paris, considerate of the comfort of idle afternoon strollers such as herself. The Palais Royal is a little crowded today; there are quite a few people milling around on the packed yellow sand, crunchy with bits of gravel. It is such a lovely day, clear and unusually mild for this time of the year, and the sunshine has pulled people out of their apartments.

The *pain au chocolat* is so exquisitely buttery that Louise takes all the time possible consuming it: she tears it off shred by moist shred. She sheds a few bits of the pastry's golden outer skin as she eats, which attracts several sparrows. They spar and chirp for her scraps. She watches them, content.

Unexpectedly, one of the birds flutters up onto her knee and pecks up a fallen speck of crust she hadn't even noticed and flies away in the same flicker of an instant. Still, this hiccup of time was long enough for Louise to feel the scuttle of its small feet against her.

She thinks: What a brash little creature! What does it know in its lentil-sized brain?

She twists the tiniest piece off the soft yellow middle of her confection and holds it out on her fingertips. She makes herself as still as she can manage. The only movement she feels in her body is her breath, slow and deep.

The sparrow, now leaning forward on the edge of the stone fountain, cocks its head inquisitively at her. It takes a springy hop forward. It gathers all the courage in its pea-sized heart, and flies onto Louise's hand. She can feel the heat of its tiny toes on her fingers, the prick of its minuscule claws. The animal plucks the crumb from her grasp and flies away. The woman almost laughs with delight.

She looks up and is instantaneously startled by a silhouette that cannot yet be familiar to her, but is. The man Langlais is walking straight for her: she can see him through the fountain's jet of water. Does he see her?

He sees her; he raises his hand in greeting. He even gives a tight little smile, slightly askew.

"Hello, Sir," she says jauntily.

"Hello, Madam," he answers. "Lovely day, isn't it? A bit strange for November, don't you find?"

Louise is flustered: she has this tingly feeling that somehow he has already read the letter she sent him, and somehow he already knows she was the one who wrote it. Of course, this is impossible, as she has just put her criminal message in the post a few minutes earlier.

"Unseasonably warm, yes," she says. "We are neighbors, it seems."

"Indeed, I recognized you from Friday. You were at your window."

"I trust your move went well?"

"It was fine. Nothing of importance was broken. My name is Langlais, by the way, Xavier Langlais."

He extends his hand, and she takes it. It is cool and efficient in her grasp: two swift pumps and it is gone. "Louise Brunet," she says. "You are out for a stroll?"

"Actually, I walk through here every day on my way home from work."

As he utters the word "work," Xavier gives a quick heave to the caramel-colored leather satchel he carries in his burdened hand, to display it.

"What do you do?"

"I teach literature to high school boys. I have a stack of their papers to look over tonight."

"That sounds very interesting."

He shrugs. "Not as interesting as all that. Ah, why don't I give you our calling card. We just got them in from the printer's this morning. My wife was quite delighted with them."

He reaches into his coat pocket for his wallet, and when he opens it, he fumbles. A hundred-franc bill spirals out, falls to the ground at Louise's feet. Louise reaches swiftly for it before it tumbles away, swept by some errant breeze. She hands it back to him.

"Be careful with your stray cash,"[13] she says, smirking.

"Ah, thank you," he answers, his smile slightly wider now, faintly glowing with something like genuine mirth. "I'll have to take that under advisement. Honestly, paper money is worth so little these days, Madam. Perhaps it is not even worth bending over to pick up. But thank you, in any case."

As he speaks, Louise reaches into her purse and plucks out her own calling card. They exchange their paper names soundlessly.

"Well, I should be getting on now," Xavier says as he puts his wallet back inside his coat, "but I shall have to meet your husband, and you shall have to meet my wife soon."

"And your children."

"Certainly. Enjoy the sunshine," he says, and then leaves, not waiting for her to say good-bye.

---

13. This language where every word means a thousand things! French is such a nightmare for a muddled translator such as myself. You see, Louise has indulged in punnery: "stray cash" is a play on words. The words in French: *espèces errantes.*

Espèces means "cash, paper money." It also means: "species, kind, breed."

Errantes means "stray, like a lost domestic animal." Also, it clearly has the same root as the word *erreur* ("error, mistake"), which implies that the stray animal is merely mistaken in the direction it is heading: if it only made a concerted effort, it could easily find its way home.

So Louise says "stray cash," but she also says "errant breed." She says: "Be careful with your errant breed."

What could this mean? It could refer to anything; she could even be telling him to be kind to his children. I am, of course, reaching ridiculously here since, at least for the moment, her pun plainly means nothing at all.

"See you," she calls after his departing back, her voice nearly quavering.

THE NEXT DAY (TUESDAY) Louise has to go out for a big grocery run: she has to look for some fine large piece of meat at the butcher's; she has to fill up on potatoes and carrots and onions at the produce market; she has to go everywhere.

She needs wine, and cream, and sugar, and chocolate—how could she have run out of all these things at once? What kind of wife is she that she cannot keep such necessities plentiful in her home!

All the same, it is fun to walk everywhere and chat with all the shopkeepers.

After a while, the bags get heavy. The handles start digging into the palms of her hands as she carries them down the street; she is full up, she has to go home. She has bought so many things because her father is coming over for dinner tonight and bringing his friend Pierre Cleper. She looks forward to it: Pierre is a fine conversationalist, if occasionally suffering from a wandering tongue around the ladies.

When she gets back to the front door of her building, she has difficulty pushing it open, laden as she is with all her ingredients. A smiling young man sees this and runs over, opens the door for her, and holds it as she passes through. She nods thank-you at him, and he offers to carry her bags up to her apartment. Normally, she would say no, but her arms are beginning to ache from her long shopping run. She consents.

The young man takes everything from her and follows her up

the stairs. He is tall, skinny, and darkly complexioned. He smells of bleach and sweat. He chatters to Louise in painfully shattered French about that time when he was seven years old and broke his leg. She cannot tell for sure what he is, Portuguese, maybe?

When they reach the door, he gives back all the bags and smiles widely at her, revealing that his top left canine is rotten, almost brown. "A little kiss, Madam?" he queries softly while leaning forward and pointing to his cheek with his index finger. "A little kiss, Madam," he states this time, "just right here on the cheek."

Louise hesitates for a moment at such a command, but decides that it is a reasonable fee for the services rendered. She gives him a peck on the apple of the cheek at the exact place he has pointed. He says thank you, and leaves.

Sentir et ressentir

THIS DAY (TUESDAY) XAVIER Langlais feels peculiar: he has received a curious letter. He is not particularly disturbed by it because, though the letter is anonymous, the content is not threatening. It is downright intriguing, if a bit unexpected.

He checked the mailbox on the way out to school; since the building he lives in is just around the corner from the post office, it is at the beginning of the mailman's route, and thus he receives his mail first thing in the morning. There was only one envelope, addressed to him. It felt so light that he thought perhaps there was nothing inside, but there was: just a sheet of poor-quality paper with a scrawled message from Lord Knows Whom, but clearly a woman.

The message contained the word "adultery" and, since this word does not leave him indifferent, he put the slip of paper back in its envelope and into the breast pocket of his suit jacket instead of throwing it away. All day, while he teaches, the letter stays there in his jacket, against his warm body.

HE GIVES AN INTERESTING lecture to his last class that day. He reads aloud a prose poem by Charles Baudelaire titled "A Hemisphere in a Mane of Hair." He asks the boys what they think. They say they think they like it but cannot be more specific, so Xavier tries to help them along. "The wording in this poem is such a delight. Do you see? It means so many different things—there are so many images. They blend together to be anything you like. You see right away, he says he *plunges* his face in the beloved woman's hair, as if he is diving into water. Then when he moves the hair around with his hand, he *stirs memories into the air,* thus, the smell of the hair is also memories. Isn't it odd?"

Xavier pauses for a moment, lets his eyes take in the room. One boy shrugs. One boy nods. He plows on. "And then in the second stanza, he says that he *sees* things in her hair, and *hears* things. Even better, he *smells* them. Where is he going with this? He is off somewhere. Right here, he says that his *soul travels on its perfume as the soul of other men on music!* The hair is water—and music—I am puzzled. Are you not?"

Again, he looks up. They are all quiet this time, but they are looking at him. He has a feeling they are paying attention; after all, they are good boys.

"Then afterward, look how far he travels! All this seafaring imagery in distant climes! We are invited to experience the saturated blue of water and sky, the songs of sailors, the scent of flowers, the humid heat of a tropical climate. Can you not feel it? Picture all the things your imagination can fill in when you are swept so far away. Since this poem was written probably eighty years ago, you can picture that the hull of the ship you're on is wood. Can you hear it creak as you sway on the waves? Where are you? What hemisphere is this?"

Now they are interested—he can tell. The boy who nodded

before is leaning forward in his seat and is utterly still. There is very little fidgeting in the room, and this pleases him.

"And in the penultimate stanza, what is he breathing in that *ardent hearth* of the woman's hair? Tobacco and sugar, and what else? Opium! Opium, dear boys. You are in the Orient now. You are so far that you can smell what he tells you to: *the tar, musk, and coconut oil.* But what manner of scent is this? Is the musk the glandular secretions on the woman's scalp? And this word *tar?*[14] This must be what they seal the hull of the ship with to render it seaworthy, no? But then again, this word can also mean just the substance that stiffens her collar. Perhaps he is just sniffing the back of her neck after all. Perhaps he is just here in his bedroom in France with a woman he is undressing, sniffing the back of her neck like some dog. But you can't know that, can you?"

Now that the words "woman he is undressing" have dropped from Xavier's mouth like radiant orbs of sex, every boy in the room is rapt—for what boy's ear wouldn't be caught by such a string of words? Especially from a teacher.

"Now, look at the last stanza. He says he is *eating memories.* Why? Because he is gnawing on his beloved's hair! Like some dog indeed: he eats her! And her tresses are long and black and heavy— perhaps she is an Oriental! He is making love to an Oriental—what scandal! Isn't it wonderful? Don't tell anybody."

He laughs in pure delight now, and the boys laugh with him. All these males in the room are on the same wavelength now, all these males in the room suddenly abloom with maleness.

---

14. The French word *goudron* means both "tar" and "starch."

"Who is this woman?" the teacher asks the roomful of students loudly. He has gotten himself warmed up.

"Tell us!" a boy in the back shouts.

"She is the Orient itself! She is a body issued from the Orient—an Oriental body—the Orient itself is her body—it is all blended, do you see? The Occident is male and the Orient is female, do you see? The Occident must conquer, the Occident must subjugate, the Occident must possess and shape the Orient into what pleases it! The Orient must yield its resources—for its own good! This dark and dangerous and mysterious place must be civilized. It is rightful for us. It is our duty to do so: it is our burden as true men. Such is the nature of our peculiar power."

Xavier is finished now and becomes quiet. His face is flushed to a high shade of crimson. Without realizing what he is doing, he removes his jacket and flings it offhandedly onto the back of his desk chair. The room has gotten so stifling all of a sudden. Is there something awry in the central heating system?

He leans back against his big heavy wooden desk and looks at his class. They have been aroused into a stunned silence by his lecture, though it is entirely possible that they didn't understand most of it. There is nothing more to say, but this is all right. He has to assign them a new novel to read for next week. Since they are studying the nineteenth century, he was thinking of giving them some grinding, plodding novel by Victor Hugo. He has suddenly changed his mind; now that he has gotten himself all lit up over the Orient, he assigns a more obscure work: Gustave Flaubert's *Salammbô*. It is a novel set in Carthage, before Christ. It is so saturated with blood and sensuality that he suspects he might receive complaints from some of the more literate parents who are familiar with the book—possibly he might get into a little bit of hot water with the administration?

He has been a talented and reliable teacher for many years, thus his career is truly in no danger. He could always feign puzzled innocence.

Even if he were to get into trouble, for some reason he seems not to care terribly much at the moment.

[NB: This is not part of the documentation; it is just a page spread from a book.]

XVII

UN HÉMISPHÈRE
DANS UNE CHEVELURE

Laisse-moi respirer longtemps, longtemps, l'odeur de tes cheveux, y plonger tout mon visage, comme un homme altéré dans l'eau d'une source, et les agiter avec ma main comme un mouchoir odorant, pour secouer des souvenirs dans l'air.

Si tu pouvais savoir tout ce que je vois! tout ce que je sens! tout ce que j'entends dans tes cheveux! Mon âme voyage sur le parfum comme l'âme des autres hommes sur la musique.

Tes cheveux contiennent tout un rêve, plein de voilures et de mâtures, ils contiennent de grandes mers dont les moussons me portent vers de charmants climats, où l'espace est plus bleu et plus profond, où l'atmosphère est parfumée par les fruits, par les feuilles et par la peau humaine.

Dans l'océan de ta chevelure, j'entrevois un port fourmillant de chants mélancoliques, d'hommes vigoureux de toutes nations et de navires de toutes formes découpant leurs architectures fines et compliquées sur un ciel immense où se prélasse l'éternelle chaleur.

Dans les caresses de ta chevelure, je retrouve les langueurs des longues heures passées sur un divan, dans la chambre d'un beau navire, bercées

par le roulis imperceptible du port, entre les pots de fleurs et les gargoulettes rafraîchissantes.

Dans l'ardent foyer de ta chevelure, je respire l'odeur du tabac mêlée à l'opium et au sucre; dans la nuit de ta chevelure, je vois resplendir l'infini de l'azur tropical; sur les rivages duvetés de ta chevelure, je m'enivre des odeurs combinées du goudron, du musc et de l'huile de coco.

Laisse-moi mordre longtemps tes tresses lourdes et noires. Quand je mordille tes cheveux élastiques et rebelles, il me semble que je mange des souvenirs.

Une femme dévergondée comme ça

THIS DAY (STILL TUESDAY) Louise has spent all afternoon working hard to prepare a beautiful meal. She serves it to three men, all mustached jewelers: her father, her husband, and their friend Pierre Cleper. The first course is fennel soup. They sip from their spoons and chat.

"Why do you not marry?" Louise's father demands to know of Pierre, in a bemused tone. "You really ought to—think of all the widows and lonely girls in our ailing nation! There are so many women, and not enough men left to give them all children."

"Why, it is precisely because of the sheer number of widows and lonely girls that I do not marry," Pierre declares. "You cannot expect me to give up such plentiful hunting grounds!"

"You are a cad!" Louise laughs.

"Yes."

They all snicker. Louise watches the curve of Pierre's lip as he blows gently onto his spoonful, to cool it. He sucks the soup into his mouth and swallows, and then asks Louise's father: "And you? Why do you not get married? Surely a widower is entitled to have one of the widows, no?"

"Perhaps, but I am done with marriage myself. Besides, I need only one woman, and that is my little Louisette!" As he says this, he reaches across the table for his daughter's hand and presses the top of it briefly. She looks at him for a moment, and makes a visible effort to smile at him.

"Once was enough, eh?" Henri asks him, with a mixture of joshing and genuine curiosity—curiosity because the man seldom discusses his dead wife (and never his dead son).

"I suppose." he answers softly.

"And you want me to do this to myself why?" Pierre asks, then turns to Louise: "Not that women aren't wonderful, but I am afraid that I am not suited for any one woman, you see."

"Well, that might be for the best. I cannot think of one woman who would find you suitable," she answers mockingly.

"She is a pistol, that one!" Pierre says to Henri, pointing to Louise with his trigger finger, as she gets up and clears the emptied soup bowls from the table. As she walks to the kitchen, she hears her husband declare, with pleasure and pride, "That's why I married her."

In the kitchen, she readies the next course by putting it in serving dishes. It is a *boeuf bourguignon* with potatoes, Henri's favorite. She likes the three men together; her father and Henri and Pierre have a certain chemistry. When they come together, they always laugh a lot and have conversations that border on the improper. Louise knows that this is because of the addition of Pierre. She thinks he is marvelous and always likes seeing him, but she knows that he would weary her if he stayed too long. Seeing her father and Henri without him is a more sedate experience—not as lively, and entirely decent.

She reflects that it is slightly unusual that her life should be so crowded with men, considering the excess of postwar women that they were just discussing. She is lucky. She knows this. She loves feeding the three of them, having them to herself.

She brings out the potatoes first in a big bowl and then comes back with the stew in a large white tureen ornamented with painted blue curlicues, the serving spoon firmly planted inside.

"Ah," Henri sighs contentedly. "Darling, it smells delicious."

She smiles and puts her culinary opus in the middle of the table. The men wait for her to sit, and Henri begins to serve everyone: first Pierre, then his father-in-law, then Louise, and last himself.

For a minute, they eat silently. Everything is precisely the correct texture: the peeled potatoes split apart under the pressure of the fork; the beef shreds in the mouth, from the mere wiggling of the tongue. The vegetables are soft, but not flaccidly overcooked.

"This dish is wonderful. It warms the heart," Louise's father says. She blushes at his florid compliment.

"Yes, a toast to the cook," Pierre says, and raises his glass. The other two men repeat his gesture, and they all sip from their wine. It is a deep, rich Burgundy, naturally, to match the main course.

The conversation begins to flow again but is more subdued: the main dish demands a greater portion of everyone's attention than the soup. They thoroughly devour the contents of the tureen, and Louise is surprised: she had counted on having some for her lunch tomorrow. She will have to think of something else to eat.

They sit in a satisfied haze until her father asks if there is any cheese.

"I have a Camembert," Louise says, "but are you sure you want some? I made a custard for dessert. Do you have room for all this?"

"Oh, I will not spoil my appetite for your custard, dear girl—I just want a tiny sliver of your Camembert, please."

She clears everything and comes back with the cheese and a small basket of baguette slices. Her father is the only one who eats. The rest of them are saving room for dessert.

The dessert is a heavy chocolate custard, a marvel of cream and eggs and decadence. A little of its smoothness goes a long way, a good long way. They savor this sweet in complete silence, and sigh in abject surrender when they are done. "Oh, Louise, your custard has finished me off," Pierre announces drowsily, dabbing his mouth with his napkin. "You're going to kill us all with deliciousness."

"Why, thank you. This makes me glad."

"I know! You are a corrupted woman like that."

After Pierre utters this, he smiles widely at her, and once again she blushes. Henri shoots Pierre a sideways glance of faint disapproval: his friend is often unchecked this way when he is sated after a good meal. Being full loosens him.

Louise leaves the men to digest at the table and smoke cigarettes while she does the dishes. She is happy that she has given them all such pleasure with this lovely meal she crafted so carefully; it took her a good six hours to put everything together. This is all right, as truly this is her primary duty in life—the feeding of men. There is also housecleaning, but cleaning is very dull. Fortunately, she has the monetary means to order a maid to come in for a few hours and relieve her of this tedious womanly chore every once in a while.

The laundry is not too bad: she takes it in to a cleaner. All she has to do is take it home and put it away within the softly sliding drawers of her husband's dresser, within the smoothly hinged doors of her armoire.

As her hands plunge mindlessly into the warm sudsy water, Louise thinks about her lone student, Garance. The girl is coming over on Thursday afternoon, and she is looking forward to it even more than usual. Thursday is the girl's birthday, and Louise has gotten Garance a present she certainly will like. It might even earn Louise an ecstatic hug from her squealing, fluttering pupil—this pupil who has such bizarre and compelling relationships with her instructors.

Louise thinks of the disdain she herself had as a young girl for her teachers, always trying to mold her into something they had neither the courage nor the talent to be. She had not obliged them by being anything as crass and unsettling as a prodigy: banality is a cozy and comfortable place. These days, she has grown downright fond of teachers and teaching; she has to, having turned into an inadvertent teacher herself.

Also, Xavier Langlais is a teacher, and though she knows nothing of the man, she is convinced that he is as fascinating as he is handsome. She feels a vague itch to hear his thoughts on literature. She thinks it must be pleasant for Mrs. Langlais to be married to a teacher: they come home earlier than most other working men, being confined only to the school day.

Even so, they must have to bring their work home fairly often, and this might be a bother.

As Louise finishes splashing around with her dishware and begins wiping it dry on a clean, rough hand towel, she can hear the men talk peacefully from the dining room but cannot distinguish their actual words. She knows that they talk about different things when she is not in the room. She suspects that these things are more explicit than what they are compelled to say in front of her. She is so intrigued—she wants to know what they say when they are alone.

Maybe, one day, she will just get up the gumption to ask: Do you talk about women? Do you talk about love? Do you talk about sex? Graphically? Do you tell one another what we do that you like very much, what feels good to a man?

To imagine her father speaking of such things to her husband! Probably they do not. She is willing to wager that Pierre talks about these things with somebody, though, even if it is neither of her two men.

She wonders also: when men are alone and unafraid to hurt the delicate ears of tenderhearted ladies, do they talk about the war?

Paris
March 18th

Dear Sir,

I am much better. I can breathe freely. I can keep food down. I am almost entirely myself again, except that sometimes this liquid heat bursts into the pit of my chest and propagates outward into my whole body, down into my hands especially, down to the quivering tips of my fingers. It is strange, for fever is usually the least persistent part of an illness, yet I cannot shake this one. It keeps exploding into my blood and brings with it the most vivid waking dreams.

Sometimes I talk to myself when I am alone. Sometimes I startle myself with the sound of my own voice at unexpected moments.

I try my best to keep myself together.

Do you recall the postcard of the group of men in puttees that I scanned for you with my first letter to you, Sir? The one with the black dog in the foreground. This one:

Most peculiar: before I went to work yesterday morning, I felt this irresistible urge to pocket the card. I did. I wore it in my suit jacket all morning, and when I passed Josianne's desk on the way to my office, I took it out and touched her shoulder with it. I had absolutely no intent to do this; after all, she had given no signs of friendliness since she'd come to my house that strange day, had not even asked if I was feeling better. It was as if I had made the gesture with no volition at all, as if my fearful resistance itself had fueled it. She looked up at me and asked me what I wanted, and I was confounded. I just stood there with the card in my hand, displaying it dumbly to her. She took it from me, beheld it for a moment, and said:

"C'est drôle comme les anglais sont pimpants et efféminés."[15]

"Pardon?"[16]

"Les français portent les uniformes clairs. Les anglais sont en foncé."[17]

"Comment savez-vous ça?"[18]

She shrugged when I asked her this. She mumbled something about having been with a historian once, and handed the card back to me. She didn't ask me where I had gotten it. She went back to her typing. I slipped the card into my pocket, and as I did so, there was a queer crackle in my head like radio interference that made me think that I must have hallucinated the entire incident, but as I walked away I heard her voice: "Si vous avez d'autres trouvailles, vous pouvez certainement me les montrer, Trevor."[19]

---

15. "It's funny how the Englishmen are dapper and effeminate."
16. "Pardon?"
17. "The French wear the light uniforms. The English are wearing the dark ones."
18. "How do you know this?"
19. "If you have other finds, you can certainly show them to me, Trevor."

I looked at her, a not-unpleasant shiver sliding down the back of my neck. Her hair flamed red like a beacon and she was smiling. I was utterly flustered, so flustered in fact that I asked her in a tumble of uncontrolled words if she would have coffee with me after work. She considered the idea for a moment and then waved me off with an airy "Non, non—pas encore . . ."

Not *yet?* Whatever could that mean?

Ah, my apologies, Sir—this is unrelated to my studies. Findings:

1. one pair of mesh church gloves, black.
2. one pair of mesh church gloves, white.
3. photograph of a young man in uniform, unidentified.
4. one gold cross pendant, large (almost as long as my little finger).
5. one silk handkerchief.

As I take my leave, I might as well offer you another one of those great groveling greetings:

En vous remerciant d'avance et dans l'attente et l'espoir de vous lire, veuillez agréer mes salutations les plus chaleureuses,[20]

Trevor Stratton

Trevor Stratton

---

20. *Thanking you in advance and in the expectation and hope of reading you, please agree to my warmest salutations*

Au nom du père et du fils

THESE GLOVES—THEIR UTMOST DELICACY, the craftsmanship of
their lacework, the fact that they are still structurally sound after all
these years of silent stillness tangled in this uncanny record, sound
enough that you could slip them on without ripping them if your
hands were small and slim enough, if your hands were the same size
as the phantom hands implied here: those of Louise Brunet, born
1896—

These gloves haunt you.

But let us not be bothered with that now. Let us not slip onto our
own body these accoutrements of the dead. Such a gesture would be

a bit strange, a bit unsettling. Such a gesture is unnecessary when the object is before us and we can look at it at our leisure.

The gloves are flexible, strong, starkly black. They look like something to be worn to the funeral of a beloved someone; as you might have observed, they look like a widow's gloves. The truth is that they are merely church gloves, worn every Sunday to holy offices. The color is so because white gloves are better suited to a virgin (or at the very least, a young and unmarried woman who could still plausibly undergo such a pantomime of purity). Black is the color of the true woman, one burdened with keeping a house and bearing children—a wife.

Louise has yearned keenly for the fulfillment of motherhood. She has been trying so hard. As of the day where our story hovers (Tuesday, November 6, 1928), she has not succeeded in this strenuous endeavor, though Lord knows she has been the most efficient puller of husbandly seed she has been allowed to be.

The gloves are mesh so that they can be comfortably worn on a warm day. Also, the hands can be seen through them. Though this effect might look sensual, this is not the true meaning of this tight netting. The idea is to let a little bit of the moist skin of the wearer's fingers through the gloves so that she can gain purchase on the pages of her prayer book as she flips them during mass.

Fingers truly gloved would slide, would force the wearer to struggle noisily with her text during holy offices, and this cannot be. What if the wearer of such gloves got frustrated with her unwieldy and tenuous grasp on her blessed book? What if she were to sigh and grumble aloud in church? This cannot be—oh—she might even forget herself and take the Lord's name in vain!

The stone church is God's house, and must be treated as such. The mesh gloves are the most appropriate, though some of the more sin-minded men in the congregation might be inclined to leer at the sheathed hands of women clasping the Book and think of what it might be like to have the mesh graze their skin, with the heat of the woman's hand still palpable through it. How wrong they are to think of taking the woman's hand in their own, pushing the lace-bordered elastic back from the wrist and kissing its underside, just at the juncture with the palm, such a sensitive and ticklish place.

Women titter when they are kissed there. They blush and look away, shivery with goose bumps.

The men are wrong to think this—in church no less.

And Louise, that corrupted woman, is even more lewd than any of these men to think of them doing such things to her in church, yes, in church.

It is not her fault: she finds the gloves irritating. It is still a bit of a trick to flip the pages with them, especially noiselessly the way she's supposed to. Bare hands would be much easier, but she cannot break with tradition. She wears the required dainty hat too, of course: a black one, since her favorite (the violet one) is too brightly colored for a place where Latin is spoken.

She finds the gloves irritating, so she sits there as this dead foreign tongue that is supposed to transport her closer to God slides past her ear, and she pictures possible contexts in which the gloves might be pleasing to her.

(Or pleasing to him—whoever the man is. To be taken in the confessional booth: her whole body quakes in heated desire at the idea. Let God strike her dead! No, let God enter her and do what

He will with her: let Him inflict His just punishment! She can use a little discipline; such a wayward child she is. Oh, to be taken in the confessional booth, but by whom? The priest? Oh no, not the priest. He wouldn't know what to do with her. Any good-looking man will do, any man who knows how to properly wield the marvel that God has given him, as long as this man has a beautiful mouth for her to kiss.)

These days, she does not go to church often because she gets bored so easily by the interminable chanting—all the standing and the sitting and the kneeling—the kneeling especially makes dirty things spring to her mind—this naughtiness always happens to her. She can't help it.

STILL, THE BLACK GLOVES may be church gloves, but she has also worn them to funerals. She's had the gloves for many years: they are expensive and beautifully made, meant to last as long as a woman's hands will fit into them, if birthing her children does not make her too fat. (The funerals: first Camille, then her brother. At Camille's funeral, she wept and wept in her father's arms; at her brother's, her heart was too exploded for her to even make a sound. If her father had tried to touch her to comfort her, she would have violently recoiled. The first time, the pain was so terrible that she'd thought it could not possibly get any worse. The second time, the pain had eaten her whole, had incorporated her into its being. Her flesh was pain itself.)

Fortunately she does not think of the gloves primarily in this context since they are such quotidian objects, yet the dim possibility remains that her reluctance to go to church and wear those gloves has something to do with her brother's funeral—

he who lived through the war

he who suffered through such long and absurd butchery only to be taken by disease—by what they call Nature—

an act of God

and what a neglectful and thoughtless act it must be for Him

like it is for us to inadvertently drop small change out of our pockets

trivial coinery

stray cash—

He, the blessed Father, doesn't even turn His head to glance at the tiny sound we make

against the hard ground as we fall.

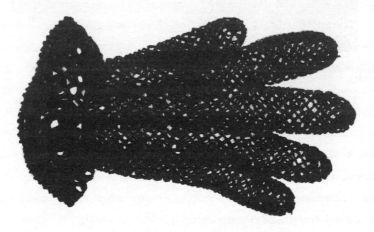

Where are we now? We've returned to this fragmented place where our line breaks.

Let us gaze then upon sweeter things. Let us gaze upon a virginal and happy past. Let us see the hands of Louise Brunet when she was still a child, before she was plagued by so much as her first menses:

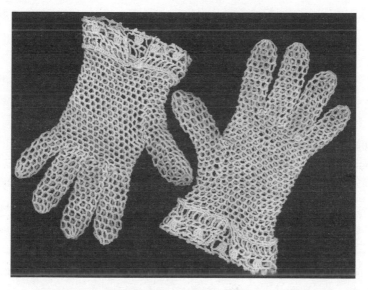

[NB: Can you see my ghostly handprints on the scanning bed? I attempted to remove them, but they would not budge. But perhaps my hands cannot be seen. Pay no attention.]

THESE ARE THE GLOVES Louise wore to her First Communion, these and a frothy white dress with a crinkly half veil that tickled her sweaty forehead. She felt lovely in her lacy clothes, all aglow and about to enter the next stage of her life—like a bride.

Her grown-up self remembers the physical details well, the slow shuffle up the center aisle with the other white-gowned girls. She remembers a vague anxiety about not receiving the wafer correctly.

Somehow she pictured her tongue fumbling the Body of Christ and the sacrament falling to the ground, defiled. She cannot remember faith, though; she cannot remember if she had this feeling of faith back then. She is not sure that the comfort of this benevolent God ever existed now, though certainly it must have. What reason would she have had not to believe? The lack of a mother?

Her brother was there that day. He was twelve years old, just beginning to show an adolescent gawkiness. His voice had not begun to crack. He watched her from the pew, and when she looked back at him standing there, with his hands together as if in quiet reflection, he puffed out his cheeks and crossed his eyes in an attempt to make her lose her composure in this most holy of moments.

As fast as his funny face came, it was gone; he was swift in order not to be caught by their father standing next to him. The speed of this flash of levity was the funniest thing about it, and Louise cracked a smile. She somehow managed not to laugh.

After they returned home, Louise struck her brother on the side of the arm with the small white Bible the priest had given her after her first confession. "You're not supposed to make people laugh in church!" she shouted.

"Maybe so, but now you have a sin ready to confess for next week."

"What's that?"

"Striking your own brother in anger with the Word of God. That's not very Christian."

Louise looked at the book still in her hand and felt like a very naughty girl, though she was pleased with herself too. The two of them, still in their church clothes, giggled as quietly as they could so as not to arouse the curiosity of their father in the next room.

IN THE RECORD WE find a picture of a young man in uniform, fading from the edges in. He is dashing but not identified. There is no way for us today to know who he is, now that everyone is dead. He bears a family resemblance to the father, so this could indeed be the son, Louise's brother.[21] Who knows: a lot of the men pictured in the record look like kin. The young man could also be Louise's cousin Camille, the one who became her beloved. He might have sent her this photograph of himself from the front lines as a token of his romantic love, like the flowery lacy postcard and like the bullet pencil case. There is no way to know.

---

21. His name is not in the record. His death is not in the record. It is as if he never existed.

The young faded man was still alive on January 2, 1916—whoever he was. On this day, Camille was on leave but had to head back out for the front lines the next day. His marriage proposal had already been turned down by Louise's father, who'd exploded in violent anger at the idea of her marrying her own blood. It simply wasn't right, he said. It was an insult to what was proper.

The disapproving father could not prevent them from being together on this day, as tied up as he was on the front lines. He was not on leave then, and could not keep Camille away from the small, cozy bedroom where Louise stayed at their aunt Marie's house in the town of Malakoff—Aunt Marie whose husband and sons were also at war, and who was not home at the moment.

Camille and Louise sat on the bed together. They had never been in such a situation before. They'd held hands and stolen kisses the last time he was home, in passing thrilling moments when they were left accidentally unchaperoned. But now they were truly alone, in a soft, warm, safe place.

They sat a foot apart, looking into each other's faces. Camille's blue eyes were filled with some sort of supplication that Louise could not reach, some sort of thing that the experience of war had etched onto his young face, making it older but still beautiful. She put her hand palm down on the coverlet between them, and he covered it with his own, stroking the back of her fingers with his trembling thumb. The contact was so warm and so strangely powerful that Louise almost wished it would stop.

"I'm frightened," Camille said. "I feel I might die."

Louise was wounded by these words and reached for him. She cupped his face, stroked his cheek, and said, "Don't speak like that. I know you will come home."

Camille seized her in his arms and pressed her to him, crushing her. She yielded immediately to this embrace, to the long, hard kiss he took from her. They breathed hard together; her lips parted slightly, and she felt the flick of his tongue pass between them. Her body shuddered in surprise and delight at this impingement. This was new; it was deeper than before, and they had some time together now, and no one knew where they were.

The kiss didn't stop. Louise's hands stroked the back of Camille's closely cropped head, and his traveled up from her waist along her back. They cradled her neck. He pushed her down and back onto the pillow and she moaned slightly at this without pulling her lips from his. His mustache tickled her and she laughed. Her giggle caused him to pull away and look at her flushed face. Their bodies were tense with expectation, pressed together on Louise's narrow bed with the crisp white sheets. He reached for her throat and unfastened the first button of her shirt, then the next.

"My father won't let us marry," she said softly, not sure whether she was protesting his clear intent to undress her.

"We will marry," he answered. "As soon as this horrid war ends, we will run away and do it and when we come back as man and wife, they will have to accept us."

"Oh—I hope so."

Her dreamy voice encouraged him, and he bent to kiss her neck. He cupped her breast with an eager and brave hand her back arched. The heat of skin through clothes was nearly unbearable to them both. Louise knew that Camille would make love to her if she let him; she was straining with desire for this. She ached warmly for something she'd never had, and though she had been told that it would hurt the first time, she did not care. She wanted so much to give herself to him.

But she was too afraid; she was too afraid of the fertility of her womb. What if he made her pregnant? She was gripped by a sudden nausea at this thought and groaned with pain when she felt his hand reach under her skirts—his febrile, trembling hand seeking to take possession of her just once before being again forced to carry a gun.

"No," she said loudly, almost weeping.

For a moment, they did not move. Then Camille sighed. "Oh, Louise."

"When we marry . . . ," she began and trailed off. He took his hand away from beneath her skirts, and for several minutes they cuddled together on the small bed, entwined and silent. Camille nuzzled the side of her neck and stayed there, breathing in the scent of her disheveled hair. She let him fondle her breast, then follow the smooth curve of her collarbone with his finger. He touched the gold crucifix tucked behind her partially open collar. It was a large piece of jewelry, with a fully rendered Jesus on one side.

"Is it because of this that we cannot make love now?" he asked of the cross, its metal warmed by her skin.

The question bit fiercely at Louise's heart, and she wondered if he meant to hurt her with it. She decided that he was in earnest when she saw his eyes, so lost and boyish. It was difficult for her to imagine the sweet and befuddled young men in her life—her cousins and her own brother—as soldiers. And the men who were old enough to be prepared for a battlefield, like her father, such men were too old to fight. There was no suitable age, but no matter. They all served anyway.

"You know I'm yours," she whispered. "You know you'll have me."

"All right," he said, looking for some measure of happiness in this promise. To seal it, he decided to give her a present, though he hadn't thought of doing so until just that moment. He sat up and reached for a thing in his pants pocket, and pulled it out slowly. He presented to Louise a delicate silk handkerchief, with flags and military drums painted at its four corners.

"My father gave this to me for luck on the battlefield. I think you should have it to remember me by. It's an important piece of my family," he said as he pressed it into her palm.

She looked at the cloth unfurled there, so thin and nearly transparent, and felt that she should refuse the gift—that to take it from him would be ill luck somehow, since it was intended to preserve him from harm.

"Are you sure?" she asked gently.

"Yes. When I make love to you on our wedding night, you can give it back to me."

She wanted to believe in this eventuality so much. She wanted to have faith in the inevitable union of their flesh more fiercely than she ever wanted religion, but she was not sure that she could manage this thing, this blind and confident love.

She was nineteen years old and he was twenty, and though they did not know this yet, Camille would never make love to Louise.

This crucifix was given to Louise by her father after her confirmation in the year 1908, now that she was a true woman before the Lord. The engraving was done by his newest apprentice, Pierre Cleper, who seemed to have a genuine gift for it. He had not yet taken on the apprentice Henri Brunet at that time—at that time before the whole world exploded around them.

It is a big piece of jewelry that the young Louise wore with great pride, but the adult Louise—the Louise who sleeps now on this night between Tuesday, November 6, 1928, and Wednesday, November 7, 1928—this Louise thinks the cross is too big. She doesn't want to be this showy with religion; the performance of it at that level makes her uncomfortable. The feel of the gold warming up against her skin would seem to be an accusation of the unbelieving heart inside her, this heart that takes such pleasure in petty sin like telling false sex stories to startled priests.

The heat of the metal against her skin might remind her too much of what she turned away: the feel of him, just once.

Her heart ails, and sometimes she lets herself know it, like on this morning of Wednesday, November 7, after she sends her husband off to work on a breakfast of tea and fresh croissants from the bakery downstairs. Now that she is alone in the house, she goes to her jewelry box to look through her small treasures.

She starts, of course, with this gift from her father, engraved so well by Cleper:

Then she works her way down to the most secret compartment of the box, seldom visited: a sliding drawer at the bottom. On the red velvet lining rests a large key. It is the key to a farmhouse near the small city of Bracieux, about two hundred kilometers from Paris. Her husband, Henri, grew up in this farmhouse, and sold it after the death of his widowed mother last year, not wanting any further entanglements with the property. Louise is not sure why, but she kept a copy of the key, as if she could not completely let go of owning the house though it was never really hers in the first place. All her life, she has lived in towns and cities with her jeweler men, but she fancies some pastoral version of herself at one with the warm earth, milking cows and tending chickens and being able to smell the rain before it comes to water the thirsty crops.

The house was sold to a Parisian couple much like themselves, except with a little more money. They use it as a summer getaway. The adjoining land was sold to the surrounding farmers, glad to extend their arable property. The farmhouse is a farmhouse no longer: on its truncated piece of land, it lies empty most of the year, and is rustic and picturesque when called to be so by its owners during warm and lazy months.

The key to this house is not rightfully hers, and it delights her to have it.

In the same compartment is folded a gossamer thing that is hers and hers alone. She takes this thing gingerly out of the small drawer and unfolds it slowly in her palm. She looks at it, puts it up to her face, smells it. It smells of nothing these days; it carries not a remnant of the man who gave it to her.

She wishes that she'd let him inside her that day. Yes, she wishes that he might have filled her with his seed that day, and that she might have borne a bastard child from her own cousin. From their intense, young, ill-advised love. It would have been a son, she is certain—a son with her own last name, her cousin's name, her father's name—a son so tightly bound to her by blood that she would not have been able to tell him apart from herself, from them all. She would have loved him so much, it would have made her ill. It would have fulfilled her womanhood utterly.

There was no way for her to know this, then—that this day was her one chance to make such a son. There was no way to predict a blank-shooting husband.

She presses the handkerchief against her heated face years later and breathes deeply. Years later, she wants to weep but does not.

Ma chère Muse bien-aimée

THE JEWELRY BOX HAS been shut up and put away. Louise decides to have scrambled eggs for lunch. The fresh eggs are cool to the touch, and their smoothness has something about it like skin. It must be the pinkish beige of their curved shells.

They are satisfying when cracked. Louise likes the crunch of the shell, the slight resistance of the film immediately beneath it when the egg is pried open, runny translucent flesh plopping and sizzling into the frying pan.

As the eggs cook, a wail rises in the distance, then another one closer, and a third closer still. Every first Wednesday of the month at noon, the air raid sirens in Paris are tested. This precaution seems appropriate, given the slippery shape of the world; one can never know what might come roaring over the horizon. The sirens scream in concert, obliterating all other sound, and Louise hums along with their one note[22] of alarm deep in her throat, as if responding to their musical greeting.

---

22. Today, across time, I sing this note, and I wish I knew music. I wish I could tell you which one it is. It is frightening and a little mournful. I close my eyes and feel the vibration in my throat. Today a Wednesday, noon.

LATER, LOUISE IS COMING home from the butcher's, where she has just bought a chicken. She is pushing open the front door to her building when she hears someone calling her. "Madam!"

Louise looks up the narrow street, searching for the voice shouting, "Madam! Wait! Let me help you."

She recognizes the dark-skinned young man immediately and inadvertently smiles. "Ah, it's you again."

"Yes, me again." He stretches out his hands. "I help you?"

Today she has only one bag and doesn't need the help. Still, she decides to humor the boy and hands it to him. If he repeats this game tomorrow, then she will refuse him. He follows her up the steps to her front door, quietly this time. When he hands her the bag, he looks solemn, and she is surprised. What of his request for the kiss on the cheek?

"Madam," he says, reaching fumblingly into his pocket. "Help me, please?" He takes out a pad and pen and holds them out to her. "Help me?"

"Help you with what?"

"To write, in French. I cannot write in French."

This is such a peculiar request that she is intrigued. She loops the handle of her bag around her forearm to leave both hands free, and asks, "To write what?"

The boy blushes. He can hardly get the words out of himself. "I love a girl. A French girl. I must tell her. I have to . . ." He offers her the pen. "Help me?"

As interesting as this development is, she is not about to let this boy into her apartment, so she sits down on the landing with the pad on her lap. The boy sits next to her at a respectful distance, though she can still smell the bleach and sweat on him. His foot is fidgeting and he keeps both hands together and pressed tightly between his knees. "So you love this girl very much?" Louise asks.

"Yes, very much, Madam."

"Well, ah, what does she look like?"

"She has blue eyes. Brown hair. She is little. She smells like . . ." The boy cannot find a word; he gestures a bloom with his hand.

"Like flowers," Louise fills in.

"Yes, like that. She has skin soft and white, and a voice like . . ."

"Like music."

"Yes, like that. Her eyes, they are filled with secrets. I want to know them. I am nothing much, but I love her more than anything. Help me?"

His gaze is so wide and earnest that it pinches something soft in her. She is fairly certain that his romantic aspirations are doomed. Nevertheless she has settled on doing this favor for him. "I'll write a letter, all right? And then you can copy it however you like," she says.

"Yes, thank you so much, Madam. You are so kind."

For a few minutes, the two of them sit on the stairs while Louise's hand races across the page in a slanting sloppy handwriting that any teacher would disapprove of. When she is done, she signs her maiden name on the bottom, with a flourish. She is not sure why she does this, but it makes her feel good. She hands the boy the pen, then presents the notepad over her arm, as a waiter would display a menu in a posh restaurant. The boy clearly does not recognize the gesture, as he doesn't smile when he takes the pad from her. He offers her his hand to help her stand up and she takes it. The boy hugs the pad to his chest and says, "Thank you so much. Thank you, Madam."

He darts quickly forward, plants a small kiss on her startled cheek, and barrels down the stairs without saying anything further. She watches him go, then shuts her door softly behind her as she enters her apartment, as if she doesn't want to disturb the remnants of the strange moment she just had.

As LOUISE COOKS, THE words from the letter she has written today swim in her head. She cannot get them out. They swirl in spirals, fluttering like leaves in the wind, and their rustling will not leave her alone. When the chicken is broiling in the oven, she sits at the dining table with the small pad of mulch paper on which she writes her grocery list. She is thinking of something too stupid to say aloud, or even to write down. What a girl she is! She feels no older than Garance.

She smiles as she thinks of the words of the letter she wrote for the foreign boy in the stairs:

My dear beloved Muse,

Each day I look at you, and each day I see the incarnation of my most incensed dreams in the body of an angel—a diabolical angel indeed, that hides the secrets of a closed heart behind her limpid eyes. If only I could dive into the azure of your eyes, I would never come out again. I would be the happiest drowned man on earth!

My beloved, your perfume enthralls me. Let your fatal flower bloom and envelop me with its scent, and I would never again need to smell another odor. Speak to me, tell me your secrets, your desires, your joys, and I would never again need to hear another music.

Your skin white and soft like daisy petals haunts my maddest dreams, my happiest fantasies. I need you, my angel. I am nothing much, but I love you more than my blood—impure and incinerated with want. You are the jewel of my life.

Louise Victor

She wants to laugh at this, but at the same time, she wants to curl up, wrapped in sadness. The fire of this overwrought feeling—this constant feeling of the animal self caged and unable to run free—she thought that this feeling would wane after the end of the war, after the first flame of her youth faded. It is not so. She is still not an adult, and this bothers her. She used to think that the birth of children would bring her peace and composure, but now she is not so sure. She suspects that adulthood is a chimera. Even her old father, so affable and seemingly resigned to the vagaries of life, can be a roiling mass of puzzlement and hurt beneath his placid exterior. (The day her brother died—what her father did that day—she will not think of this. It is not in the record.)

All these measured manifestations, all these repressed emotions—what considerate liars we all are, being so civilized.

Louise looks at the faintly yellow paper before her and does not want to be civilized. Damn all this consideration, she thinks. She writes:

Dear Sir,

Today I think of you. I think of your beautiful mouth and what it might feel like on me. I think of your beautiful hands and what they might look like freeing me of my clothes. Your slide into me—what might that be like? What do you taste like? I'm sure you are delicious.

You eat my dreams and I don't know why. Please show me why that body of yours burns in me like a distress flare. Give me a reason to be so warm and ready for you. There has to be a reason. You must fulfill it.

There must be some room we can meet in, some room you can rent with a little bit of stray cash, some place for committing this magnificent crime.

Thanking you in advance and in the expectation and hope of reading you, please agree to my warmest salutations,

Madam

The business closing makes her titter aloud to herself—she didn't know she had such panache. She is a funny woman.

There is nothing for her to do but post this letter while she is still in this heated trance, and see if anything happens.

WHEN HUSBAND AND WIFE get ready for bed together that night, Louise says to Henri, "I wrote a love letter today."

Henri slips in between the sheets and looks her over, propped up on pillows in her white nightgown. "Oh yes?" he says. "And to whom?"

"I don't actually know. To some complete stranger. A young foreigner who couldn't write French asked me to help him write a love letter to a girl he wants."

"And you did?"

"Why not? I had time."

"It's true. One must pass the time. What did you put in the letter?"

"Oh, some nonsense about muses and flowers and music and fire in the blood."

"Sounds romantic," Henri says, with a distracted look on his face that Louise cannot read.

"If we had known each other during the war, would you have written me things like that?"

"Probably. The war did strange things to people."

Louise looks into her husband's face, softened by the light of the bedside lamp, and it occurs to her that maybe he has written things like that, to some other woman, during the war. She wants to ask him. She wants to tell him about Camille. She has a feeling that he would not be angry, but still, something stops her from saying such things. What would happen if she were to introduce stories of sweeping romance into a marriage that has none? They had come together truly as man and wife, and thoroughly. Still, their union was one made in a spirit of weariness; a wish for peace and quiet was what drove them toward each other. He worked for her father. He was a good man. She wanted a good man, something steady and safe, something unlike the blazes of the just-ended war.

For all that, such blazes sometimes flare in her heart and find no outlet.

Henri looks back into Louise's eyes and smiles gently. He lays his hand on top of hers, which is resting on the coverlet, and says, "You know, foolishness like that can feel lovely for a while, but it doesn't last. It is false."

She leans in and kisses him, kisses his lax and comforting lips. She does love him. Yet she is riddled with flaming foolishness—and she knows such things don't last, but she cannot accept that such things are false just because they are fleeting.

Ma chère Muse bien-aimée,

Chaque jour je te regarde, et chaque jour je vois l'incarnation de mes rêves les plus insensés dans le corps d'un ange — un ange bien diabolique, qui cache les secrets d'un cœur fermé derrière ses yeux limpides. Si seulement je pouvais plonger dans l'azure de tes yeux, je n'en ressortirais jamais. Je serais le noyé le plus heureux du monde !

Mon cœur, ton parfum m'enivre. Que ta fleur fatale s'épanouisse et m'enveloppe de sa senteur, et je n'aurais jamais plus besoin de sentir autre odeur. Que tu me parles, me racontes tes secrets, tes désirs, ton bonheur, et je n'aurais jamais plus besoin d'entendre autre musique.

Ta peau blanche et douce
comme des pétales de marguerite
hante mes rêves les plus fous,
mes fantasmes les plus heureux..
J'ai besoin de toi, mon ange.
Je ne suis pas grand chose.
mais je t'aime plus que
mon sang — impur et
calciné d'envie. Tu es le
joyau de ma vie.

Louise

Victor

[NB: This letter is not part of the documentation; it is just a page
spread from a book.]

THAT NIGHT, LOUISE HAS a dream that she is lost in the metro. She walks through an endless series of interconnected tunnels, the familiar white-tile maze of a station change. She can hear the trains pulling in and out of stations below her, but she cannot get to any of them, nor can she can get back up above ground. There are no signs. Only stairs that lead to more tunnels—yes, she can hear the metal screeching of rails—where is she and what is happening?

Then there is another sound, a fizz at first like static. This sound intensifies until it becomes a roar. Slowly it overwhelms the regular ins and outs of the trains. This roar—it fills her head—she can hear some sort of spiraled swirling, so fluid—

At this moment she knows that this is the sound of water, the sound of water rushing into the passages. She knows that the river Seine has somehow breached this tight and nonsensical network of tunnels she is lost in, and that the dark green roil of it is coming for her. Soon it will turn the corner with a fantastic blast of unclean foam, and she will feel the cold, and the pain of her gasp will be immense from the shock of it, from the shock of inhaling this water, this wicked and sentient water that clearly means to have her and her alone—

So afraid, she stands utterly frozen, listening. She can feel the tears gather in her at her inevitable death, at the inevitable suffering of that death. The moment she is about to be broken open by her first sob, she wakes up, smarting, eyes wide with terror.

THE NEXT MORNING (THURSDAY), Louise is on a constitutional at the Jardin du Palais Royal when she runs into Mrs. Langlais sitting on a bench, looking over her youngest boy playing by himself in the sandbox. The pale skin on the woman's round face is pinkened by the briskness of the morning. Louise likes her distracted expression; the woman looks almost like a child, sitting there erect with her coat open and her legs crossed at the ankles, slowly eating small cookies out of a white paper bag without looking at them.

Louise waves hello to the woman, who looks startled for a moment, but not unfriendly as she waves back. Louise walks to her.

"Hello," she says, "I'm your neighbor Louise Brunet? I've already met your husband."

"Oh, of course! Sit, please. Nice to meet you. I'm Pauline Langlais," the woman responds, quickly extending her hand and shaking Louise's vigorously for several seconds. The woman is warmer and less formal than her husband. Louise likes her forthright smile and her faintly electrified blond hair, rising in diaphanous wisps in the dry wintry air.

"The weather seems to have cooled off slightly," Louise observes.

"Yes, but I think it's supposed to get warm again soon. Strange, so late in the year."

The two women sit together watching Pauline's towheaded son attempting to dig some sort of tunnel through the slightly wet sand in the box. The knees and seat of his pants are darkened by moisture, his face flushed a fierce red by his scooping efforts.

"What's his name?" Louise asks.

"This is Antoine. He's five. He'll go to school next fall. They grow so fast."

"Do they," Louise replies, without the rising inflection of a question.

"They do. The middle one is called Lionel, and he's nine, and the eldest is called Nicolas, and he's almost thirteen."

Out of nowhere, it occurs to Louise in a flash that had Camille given her a bastard child on the day she wouldn't let him make love to her on her narrow bed, the child would be about the same age as Nicolas. As if Pauline has picked up a scrap of what Louise is thinking, she reflects aloud, "It was hard being alone with Nicolas during the war. I was so frightened."

Immediately Pauline's eyes come sharply into focus as if she has just realized that she is speaking to a woman she has just met, and not a dear friend. "Oh, I'm sorry," she says.

"That's all right. What was your husband doing during the war?"

"He was a fighter pilot."

Louise is dizzied by this announcement—that tidy and exceedingly polite fellow, a fighter pilot. Some roaring ace of the sky, dashing and daring and half-crazy—what an idea! Perhaps that is why he has such an attractive confidence in the carriage of his body: he is afraid of nothing.

"You have a handsome boy," Louise remarks.

"Thank you," Pauline answers, then calls to her son, "Antoine, come here! Come meet our new neighbor!"

"In a minute. I have to finish."

"He is silly." Pauline smiles at Louise. "He's obsessed with blasting passages through the Swiss Alps for trains. Tunnels and trains, that's his thing lately."

"That's adorable."

Antoine must have heard his mother, for he shouts out a correction from his worksite. "I'm not in the mountains today!"

"Then what are you digging?"

"A tunnel under the English Channel."

"What an undertaking! That'll be the day," Louise remarks.

"Indeed. Man must assert his dominion over nature!" the boy announces, deepening his voice and raising his arms. Both women laugh.

"He gets this language from his father." Pauline smiles at Louise again. "He's prone to that sort of bombast in his lectures. He's rather appealing when he does that, in a boyish way, just like his son here. Say, would you like to meet for dinner on Saturday? You and your husband could show me and Xavier a good restaurant in the neighborhood. I think I shall like an evening among adults. That is, if you are not already engaged on such short notice."

"Oh no, that would be lovely. We are not engaged this Saturday, and we could take you to Le Poquelin, just around the corner from our building. It's very good."

"Wonderful!" Pauline's face glows with genuine delight that her spontaneous invitation was immediately accepted. "Come down to our place at eight, and you can walk us there."

"Henri and I will look forward to it."

At this moment, Antoine's tunnel silently and softly caves in on itself, and his child voice rings out, "Damn!"

"Language, Antoine!" his mother chides. "Now come over here and meet our neighbor."

The boy gets up and comes over, slapping the sand off his hands onto his trousers. "A pleasure to meet you, Madam," he says, and gives a curt bow. He is already attempting to emulate his father's formal self-possession. Louise is amused. "A pleasure to meet you as well, young sir," she replies.

The boy turns to his mother. "Can I have a cookie?" he asks, dropping his stiff demeanor.

"If you are as polite to me as you just were to Mrs. Brunet, you may have a cookie."

"May I have a cookie, please?"

"All right."

Pauline takes a small cookie from the bag on her lap and holds it out to her son. The boy leans forward and delicately grasps the sweet between his lips like an animal being fed a treat, and flicks it into his mouth with his tongue. The mother lightly touches the child's soft red cheek with the side of her index finger. "What do we say?" she asks, in a tender tone meant to mimic chiding.

"Thank you."

Louise is struck by the intimacy of the moment between mother and son. She might as well not be there at all. Indeed, it takes Pauline a few seconds to realize that Louise is sitting right next to her, and to offer her a cookie.

She accepts one and takes her leave. As she walks away, she eats the cookie. It is crunchy and buttery, with just a hint of lemon. It is so flaky that she can break it against her palate by pushing it up with her tongue. It crumbles immediately, so golden and so yielding.

TODAY IS GARANCE'S SIXTEENTH birthday and Louise is as excited as the girl herself when she hands over her gift in a plain white envelope, the two of them sitting on the piano bench together after the lesson. The present is two tickets for a production of Bizet's *Carmen* at the Opéra Garnier the very next night. Garance thanks Louise effusively and hugs her. She even plants a firm kiss on her teacher's cheek, and Louise laughs. "You can take whomever you like. A boy, even, if your parents will let you."

Garance shrugs. "Boys are dull. Are you free tomorrow night? I would rather take you. Your husband won't be jealous, will he?"

"He is not much for operas, and yes, I am free tomorrow night. I would be delighted to escort you, young lady."

Louise is happy that the girl has asked her, and has to some extent expected this. She most certainly would not have booked another engagement for that evening. She instructs Garance to wear the most beautiful dress she has: an evening at the opera is a formal affair.

The girl is opening her mouth to say something when the two of them hear an odd sound, like a distant crash. They follow this sound to the window and open it. They can see across the back courtyard into the kitchen window of the apartment directly on the other side. A plate is in sharp white shards on the floor, and a man and a woman stand over it, facing each other, their bodies tense as if ready to bolt from the room or leap at each other's throats. They are unaware that they are being watched. Louise can hear the man's voice, muffled through his shut window, ask the woman, "What did you have to do that for? My mother's china!"

"I will break another if you say it again. Say it. Go on and accuse me again." The woman's voice is strident, more audible than the man's. Louise watches as she picks up another plate from the drying rack and brandishes it. Both spectators are transfixed.

"Go ahead and smash everything in the house," the man hisses, "but I will get an answer somehow. I will know what it is that you do with Simon. I already know. Look at your face. Your mouth is so ugly when you lie."

At these words, the wife's face winces as if she has bitten into a lemon, and her hand comes down fiercely, letting go of the plate. The sound of it shattering travels perfectly to Louise and Garance crouching at the window, as if they are in the room with the couple. The pieces of crockery glide apart smoothly across the clean kitchen tile, as if on ice. There is something beautiful about the vividness of the impact and the swift spread of the wreckage at their feet. The woman screams wordlessly at this display, and leaves the room. The man follows. They continue to shout across their apartment, but their words fade away and are lost.

A scene like at the theater: a man accusing a woman of adultery. The man, cold and furious; the woman, tearful and cornered. Louise's throat seizes with anxiety at the funny coincidence of what she has just witnessed and the letter she has recently put in the mail. What if Henri found out such a thing about her? He would probably be silent and aggrieved. She would not be able to be defensive and throw things around in the kitchen. If she indulged in such violence, he might ask her if she had gone mad, if she needed to see a doctor.

She smiles wanly as she imagines her husband's puzzled expression at such a moment. Surely, he would not explode in a fury of betrayed possession and ravish her immediately all over the living room, as she imagines the furious young man is doing to the cornered wife at this very moment. She lives in a measured and reasonable marriage to a measured and reasonable man.

If she made love with another, he would be stricken to the quick. He might ask her if she wanted a divorce. She would say no. They would have to work something between the two of them. It would be a quiet disaster.

Garance turns to Louise and does not see that her teacher is restless with worry. She is merely excited at the private thing she has just witnessed. She flutters the opera tickets in her hand like a fan and says, her smile glowing with mischievous youth, "Good Lord, this is wonderful. Every time I come over to your place lately, something exciting happens."

The teacher smiles sadly to herself, her heated body awash with desire and shame, and shuts the window.

Un dispositif simple

THIS DAY (THURSDAY) XAVIER Langlais feels most peculiar: he has received yet another curious letter. It is even more explicit than the last. He is electrified by it, by this sudden intrusion of new sex into his life, especially because he has a pretty good idea now of who has written him. It is so strange: he has spoken to her only once! Why has she conceived such a storm of lust in her mysterious body for him? He does not understand, but he is not indifferent. She is not unattractive.

It must be her; he recognizes the pun in her request that he get a room to take her to—this *stray cash* she delivered with that strange little smile that afternoon on his walk home through the public garden. Surely it is a signal that she wants to be recognized. The meaningless play on words acquires meaning by being repeated in this new context, and becomes a harbinger of something enormous, some portentous and thoroughly inappropriate development in his life.

His body hums. His soul roars. The feeling reminds him of his fighter pilot days.

Yes, he, one of the first fighter pilots in the world, swooping through the sky in this war that started with cavalry charges. At first, his mission was always reconnaissance, and he was given only a revolver to defend himself. A revolver!

Was he supposed to steer his machine while making note of trench locations and shoot the pilot of an enemy plane right between the eyes, should such a plane make its sudden appearance in the air next to him? It was absurd and he knew it, but he tried not to let himself know it too acutely. He failed at this. Images of being destroyed often came to him too clearly, and he could not push them away.

Eventually, they gave Langlais a plane with a machine gun mounted on it, right in front of him for easy reach. Yet the contraption was put together oddly: the weapon was aimed right through the radius of the rotating propeller. The gun had to be calibrated to shoot between the spinning blades with each revolution. The engine had to be in perfect sync with the weapon—such delicate and dangerous engineering for his rickety, shuddering little flying machine.

Every time—every single time he went up—every time, Langlais could picture the mechanism hiccupping just once. Just this tiny failure would make him shoot himself in the most important place in the plane's body! He would go down right there, howling over enemy lines. If he didn't die in the wreckage somehow (but he had to), they would take him, and that would be even worse. The images that flooded through him were crystalline in their clarity, triggering a cold terror. It possessed his body utterly; it was almost a beautiful thing, alive and sentient like some evil animal.

Before every time he went up, he vomited. Helplessly, like some little nothing boy. He would fall to his knees as if someone had kicked the backs of them and heave all the contents of his stomach onto the ground (sometimes on all fours, bracing himself to the earth with the palms of his convulsing hands). The other pilots would laugh. They would slap him hard and manfully on the back and call him a pansy. He was so pale then, with a yellowish tinge like old paper.

Truly, the other pilots did not entirely scorn Langlais; they were even a bit jealous. They wished they could grovel on the floor and vomit, too. Pansy was not the only thing they called him; he had a nickname that was a play on his last name: *L'Angle*. The Angle. It was also a reference to the sharpness of his military posture, to his formal and polite manner. One of the men who was fond of math liked to call him Acute Angle when he said something clever, and from then on this punnery followed him everywhere. When he said something stupid, he would immediately be called Obtuse Angle.

When the mission went well and the other pilots were happy, they would take Langlais out that night and get him rip-roaring drunk. It wouldn't take much to do so: his body was already so over-wrought from what he had been through that day that it was entirely wound up. His stomach burned so hard that it shot the alcohol immediately into his bloodstream, straight to the brain before he even took a second shot of liquor. The poor fellow, his face was already crimson before he even started drinking; his circulatory system was heightened too. His florid complexion was a testament to the swiftness of his blood flow.

Because he was made so immediately drunk, he could not even get enough booze in his system to make himself sick before he needed to go to sleep. This was fortunate: a man should avoid vomiting twice in one day.

He would get so drowsy so fast that he could not even hold his head up, and his collapsed bearing made the other men laugh: their dear stiff Angle, melted like so much hot candle wax. The pilot who was fond of math would take pity on him and help him to his bunk, leave him there passed out on his small, hard bed, still fully dressed. His sleep on those nights was not to be believed: total obliteration, as if his body had flung out his very soul. There were no dreams, and when he woke up he had no idea where on earth he was, or even who he was.

But it could not be denied: on such mornings, he felt absolutely fantastic. He felt the whole world was his. His walk had a marvelous swagger of pure ownership; he struck the ground with his heels as if it should crack beneath him. To fissure the earth with every step: his aim.

Women loved this gait of his. It utterly turned their heads. They would look over his wilted uniform and ask to see his revolver. He was only too glad to oblige; he was proud of the thing. It was a smooth six-chambered affair that he kept well oiled. It spun so sweetly from being so perfectly lubricated.

—click—

"You see? This is where the bullets go in. A simple device, really. Would you like to hold it?"
—click—

OH, DO YOU SEE—HIS whole body heated with elation and want— this blaze made him forget his wife and his little boy. Some of the women eagerly accepted his offer to handle the weapon. Others were too nervous and tentative to do so.

Still, he vomited helplessly every time he had to pull up into the sky in his roaring gamble of a machine. He went up because he was made to; they ordered him and he had no choice. He was merely one of the lower links in the pitiless Chain of Command. He went up because he had to, and his body buckled in terror and fury against this inevitability, trembling and pouring forth cold sweat every single time. But after a while he couldn't stop going up, even if they'd let him. After a while, this horrid vertigo fueled his entire life. He was weak like a boy and strong like a man.

Still, the poor fellow, he was much happier when all this foolishness ended, and he was allowed to become a schoolteacher. He was good and settled then, and never again forgot about his wife and his little boy and the little boys that followed and the little girl he hopes she is carrying today.

Xavier suspects he knows whom the letter is from. Oh, with every passing moment the picture becomes clearer. He will find out soon enough if his guess is correct. His wife has told him they are having dinner with the Brunets this Saturday, and he cannot wait. He cannot wait to watch Louise's face as she sits across the table from him. Certainly she will squirm with embarrassment, with fear, with need for his body. What could be more satisfying?

To take possession of what is offered to him might be more satisfying. It would also be a bad idea. He knows that hurt of some sort must lie this way, but still, it is an interesting proposition. He has to think it over.

Dear Sir,

Do you remember the fused bullets? This object:

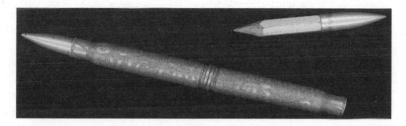

This morning, I could not go to work without it tucked in my pants pocket. I wear no jacket these days. There is an unseasonable muggy heat settling over Paris and making the air dirty and thick. I gripped it the whole way there on the metro, not sure whether I was afraid it would leap out of my pocket and do something, or whether I truly wanted it to. It did, in any case. When I passed Josianne's desk on the way to my office, I took the thing out and displayed it to her on the open palm of my sweaty hand. I could not tell for certain whether I premeditated this. I just knew I wanted her to react, somehow. I have a feeling that she has something to do with all this business.

It is funny how nothing startles this woman. She merely said: "Une autre trouvaille?"[23]

---

23. "Another finding?"

"Un objet fascinant, vous ne trouvez pas?"[24]

"Vous avez remarqué les bouts pointus? Vous savez pourquoi ils sont comme ça?"[25]

I was about to ask why she was asking such a thing when I noticed that we were answering each other's questions with questions, and I felt disarmed. I relented. "Non, pour-quoi?"[26]

"Ils signifient que les balles sont supersoniques. Ça veut dire que la balle est dans la chair avant que la cible entende la détonation."[27]

"You begin to die before you know you've been shot?" I said in English, forgetting myself.

"Yes," she answered.

"You speak English! How do you know that, about the bullets?"

She shrugged. "I was with a physicist once."

I laughed then, and said, "Do you make this a habit? I mean, are you collecting scholars of various disciplines?"

"Ça vous intéresse, Trevor, les collections de ce genre?"[28]

Like a foolish boy, I felt myself blushing to the roots of my hair. Here I had attempted to startle her, and the confounded woman had completely routed me. I said nothing and went away feeling her smile at my back, still surprised at the slight and melodious accent in her easy English. In the safe confinement of my office, I loosened my tie, took a deep breath, and decided that it would be better for me never to try to speak to that woman again.

---

24. "A fascinating object, don't you find?"
25. "Have you noticed the pointed tips? Do you know why they're like that?"
26. "No, why?"
27. "They signify that the bullets are supersonic. This means that the bullet is in the flesh before the target hears the detonation."
28. "Do such collections interest you, Trevor?"

But oh, the bullet, Sir . . .

Sometimes I feel as if I've been shot with it, clear into the heart—
so fast, so very fast that I do not even have a chance to guess what
has burned its heated metal way through my body before I am lost.

And now, findings:

1. a quickly dashed note from Camille to Louise, dated 2
   November 1915.
2. a custom-made pin displaying a portrait of Louise's
   father.
3. a license to drive a motorcycle, belonging to Henri
   Brunet.
4. a pair of photographs featuring a motorcycle and its
   sidecar.

My warmest greetings to you, Sir.

Sincerely,

Trevor Stratton

Trevor Stratton

[NB: Why is my hand so attracted to those rare letters addressed in scrawling pencil? Always I am drawn to hurried days in the life of Camille Victor—days of military happenings in which he does not have time for carefully inked curlicues. Why am I always drawn to the possibility of something dreadful happening?]

[NB: Slowly my fingers part the torn envelope and slip out this missive . . .]

At the Army, on 3-11-15

My Dear Louisette—

I write you these few words in haste because I don't have much time since we are preparing for a maneuver near

Dunkerque—for a few days, apart from that my health is good
and I think improved because of you—the Pastilles are good
for me—thank you—[29]

---

29. Oh, I am sick again. The fever burns in my face, the back of my neck, the pit of
my chest. My hands are searing hot and shaking; I feel as if they might singe whatever I touch but I must not—I must not damage the record with this unreasonable
heat in my body. The images come and I am so frightened, but it is not my fear that
I feel. It is yours. I am you on that day, November 3, 1915. We are Camille Victor,
Sergeant in the Third Infantry Battalion, Second Company, First Section.

Our company captured some Germans today. Our Captain turns to us and says,
"Let's have some fun" and we cannot fathom what the Captain means by that until
he takes one of the German prisoners, a small smooth-faced blond one. He takes the
boy out in the back, in a quiet patch of trees, and brings us along—us alone because
he likes us best out of all the company. Perhaps the Captain even loves us in a way we
do not utterly understand but we accept it and are glad of it.

The Captain holds the German by the back of the neck and throws him to the
ground, flat on his stomach. He orders the boy not to move and the boy does not. He
lies there with his hands palm down, held slightly off the ground in a gesture of surrender. The Captain whispers in our ear, "Give him a good scare—I want to watch
you give him a good scare" and he hands us his gun—his revolver, an officer's gun
that we do not ourselves have, so that it is an honor for us to touch this weapon.

We have no volition. We watch ourselves move in heated fascination. The handle
of the gun is so cold in our warm palm. We pin the German to the dirt by grinding
our knee into the boy's back. We press the barrel of the gun into the haunch of the
limp body beneath us. We run the barrel up along the spine—we take our time doing
this—and then we hold it against the back of the boy's head. Then we rest it gently
against the back of the German's downy neck so that the boy can feel the cold metal
there, against his goose-fleshing skin. Is our nauseous thrill something like delight?
It must be we are an animal, a savage, an apache—just like Father said when we beat
that boy senseless in the schoolyard who had called us a coward.

The side of the German's face is pushed into the brown loam. We can see one of
his eyes. They are held tightly shut in a gesture of negation—poor boy, to obliterate
this moment from your life, you never will. You don't want to grant us the pleasure
of seeing your terror, but we do.

We stand up now, with our feet around the boy's waist bracing his prone body on the ground. We take aim with the revolver, yes. We cock it. The dry click of that hammer is delicious. We are frightened every day and in every moment and on this day we are still frightened, but now it is almost good. It is an ecstatic fear.

Oh the Captain watches us as we discharge his weapon—yes. We quiver at the dreadful, the fantastic impact. The detonation echoes in a way that sounds as if all of us are at the bottom of a huge chasm in the ground, surrounded by rock.

We have shot the earth two inches beside the boy's skull.

The bullet hole in the packed dirt is a small innocent-looking thing, no bigger around than our little finger. It looks like the burrow of some beetle.

We glance over the boy to see if he's pissed himself, or left scratch marks in the dirt in a gripping spasm of his fingers—at that moment—the moment that we, as far as he knew, killed him.

He has not moved at all. He lies there limp, his eyes open and staring so dazedly that we briefly think perhaps the back of his head has been blown off after all.

"Shit," the Captain says wistfully. "It's better when they piss themselves."

So the Captain has done this before, this pretend execution. We can see why. It does let out some of the pressure and the German deserves it because he is German so we step off him and we kick him in the stomach and he curls and groans—he is alive after all and we are relieved—oh—what are we doing?

Camille, what have you done? It must be that something ill will come for you because of this. But of course it is not so. It is not necessary to deserve what terrible things happen to us. Guilt is not necessary when the time comes

for an execution.

[NB: In this state of vapor, I drift. From the Great War to the Greater War, I drift. I settle on this brooch made of mere base metal—but base metal was hard enough to come by when this brooch was made during the occupation.

You might recognize this face, this face duplicated from a photograph dated *26 Janvier 1943*. It is Louise's father—he makes a gift of his likeness for his daughter to wear shortly before he dies, engraved onto a dangling coin-shaped brooch by his friend Pierre Cleper. The father's vision failing and the life draining from him make it so that he must know that he doesn't have long. Strange ideas resurface. He offers his etched face to his daughter to wear on her palpitating breast.

Louise says thank you when she receives this present, and tentatively kisses her father on the cheek. The gift unsettles her a little—it reminds her of an impulse that roars deep within the flesh, hidden far within and brought to light only once, on a terrible day in December 1918. She prefers not to think of it; she prefers not to think ill of a man who is so necessary to her.

She is touched by his gesture. She loves her father so much. Yet she will never wear this brooch. She will keep it packed in a little round plastic box, a piece of cotton protecting its face. She will keep this object until her death, contained like an amulet too powerful and wicked to be used by a mere human but too sacred to be destroyed.

The creation of this object is long after the days of our story, almost fifteen years past our November 1928. Louise is already middle-aged when she tucks her father's venerable metal face into a recessed corner of her jewelry box.

In the record today, we find the brooch preserved thus:

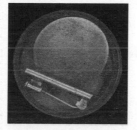

intact and sealed by her careful hands.]

Une photo de toi aussi

IN THE DOCUMENTATION IS an identification photograph of Louise's husband:

You can see that he goes by his middle name, and not his first. You can see that he bears an uncanny resemblance to Louise's father, only with a slightly broader face. In this photograph he is only thirty, but he is already half-bald, prematurely aged. Louise's father, in spite of all the grief he has suffered with the loss of his wife and his only son, is well preserved and ages slowly. It is almost as if the two men are converging through the years.

This document is a driver's license for a motorcycle, issued in Henri's hometown of Bracieux. He bought the motorcycle there too and kept it at his mother's farmhouse. He liked to give his wife and his mother turns riding in the sidecar. He liked to watch them grip their seats and close their eyes against the wind as he took hairpin turns along the dirt road.

The motorcycle was his one extravagance, purchased in the year before his mother died. It is a Harley-Davidson. Now that she is gone and the family farmhouse is sold, he keeps it parked in the courtyard of his apartment building in Paris, covered with a tarp. He has not taken it out since first putting it there; roaring through cramped city streets does not interest him. He wanted only to feel the rush of open air on the wide and empty road, like so:

This photograph was taken in the summer of 1926, from too far away. Louise did not know how to properly operate the camera. Despite this, Henri is recognizable, as is the outer edge of the town of Bracieux behind him. Henri, tightly packed into his suit, poses proudly on his reckless machine.

After Louise snapped the picture, her husband shouted to her, "Have you got it?"

"I hope so," she answered. "I can't tell. You looked so far away through the lens. I hope you come out all right!"

She should have stepped closer; she framed too much of the blankness of road and sky. But the focus is sharp enough that you can see that the man in this picture is the same fellow from the driver's license, if you look closely.

Louise put the lens cap on the camera and walked back across the dusty road. She rearranged herself, cozy and snug, into the sidecar, the camera clutched to her lap. Henri started the engine with a swift kick, and they were off again, the cooling afternoon wind blasting into their faces. The rush of air through Louise's hair felt almost like fingers brushing backward against her scalp. Neither of them wore helmets. They had no use for such impediments.

Bracieux disappeared behind them. Soon they were surrounded by fields, and the only sound they could hear was the rumble of the motorcycle. The vibration of it traveled all through the exoskeleton of the sidecar. When Henri went too fast, it felt almost as if the thing would fall apart around her, and she rather liked the thrill of it. They were so far away from everything—Henri from the small and painstaking nature of his work with jewelry, and Louise from the small and painstaking nature of her barren housewife life, her only true happiness stemming from teaching a girl who would surely outgrow her, become bored with her limited instruction and leave her, inevitably.

Down the road a piece there was a little forest, and when they reached it, Henri stopped.

"What are you doing?" Louise asked.

"I think I should take a photo of you, too."

"Ah, darling, you know I don't like to have my picture taken."

"But look, the foliage will make for an interesting background. Come on. Give me the camera."

Louise picked the camera up from her lap but stopped before she handed it off to Henri. She didn't know why, but she'd never liked having her picture taken. The dry little click of the shutter made her feel as if some small piece of her was being sliced out of her body—some irredeemable sliver of soul that she could never get back again. When she thought about how primitive this unease was, it made her smirk at herself. She had heard that African Bushmen harbored the same belief. She, so superstitious and uncivilized for no reason she could name—it was a bit funny, really.

"Oh, Louise," said Henri, "don't be fussy. Please indulge me!"

It was true; she was being fussy. What harm could there possibly be in having her picture taken on a lovely, quiet day such as this? She gave her husband the camera. Henri took it from her, took the lens cap off, and took a few steps backward down the road. He positioned himself, looking at his wife through his device as he focused it. She looked a bit forlorn there in the sidecar by herself.

"Come on now," he said. "Just give me a little smile."

Louise pulled the corners of her mouth up with the slightest twitch, and her husband pushed the button. The shutter clicked:

You can see that the photograph came out well, despite its extensive fading through the years. You can still see the texture of the grass, and even the shape of some of the leaves in the background. If you squint, you can even read the number on the motorcycle's license plate. If you squint, you can even make out the soft oval face of Louise Brunet on that fine summer day, slightly anxious at having her likeness captured but trying to look happy to please her husband.

Look now. Look now at the face of the owner of the record. After all this sifting through the documentation, we have finally pinned down her elusive gaze. She is looking at us through the lens. At this moment, she does not yet know what we already know about her.

She has just turned thirty and she still hopes that she might be pregnant soon. She thinks: this year is the year.

It is not, and neither is the year after that. But the year after that, there is the sudden appearance of Xavier Langlais, and who knows what might come of it?

The owner of the record peers at us through the jumble of the documentation. Somehow we know that once Henri has taken the picture, he feels great tenderness for his wife. He asks her, "Do you want to drive for a bit?"

Her face lights up. She does not even have to say yes for her husband to perceive her immediate glee. He lets her do this only when they are out alone in the open, because it is not entirely proper for a woman to be seen driving a motorcycle. She scrambles out of the sidecar before Henri changes his mind. He smiles at her as she takes her place. She saddles the motorcycle and kicks the engine alive with violent gusto. A metallic rush of adrenaline floods her mouth as she leans into her gathering speed.

She, flying down the road with her laughing husband at her side, unlicensed and free—dimly registering fear of wreckage, but happy.

L'amour est enfant de bohème

LOUISE IS WEARING A fringed black dress with an open V neckline tonight, Friday, November 9. She is waiting for Garance. They are going to the opera, and Henri will go out drinking with Pierre Cleper. It seems a wonderful arrangement.

The doorbell rings, and Louise walks to answer hurriedly, hoping the girl is dressed appropriately. She is, after all, sixteen, and as far as Louise knows has never been to the opera. She opens the door and is stunned.

"Garance! Where did you get that dress?"

"Uh—it was my mother's," the girl stutters. "Is it too much?"

"My dear, it is gorgeousness."

Garance is wearing a bright red satin dress, floor length, with a small train in the back. The skirt is the trumpet shape that was in fashion before the war, but the outfit is much more daring than anything Louise remembers anyone wearing back then. The shiny fabric clings to the girl's hips, and the bodice is tight and boned like a corset. It blooms open in a heart-shaped neckline that reveals Garance's pale and flawless throat. There are no sleeves, only wide straps that leave the outer curves of her shoulders unsheathed. Her thin, graceful arms are utterly bare.

"By God, turn around," Louise says.

The girl obliges, and Louise admires a row of small round satin buttons that follow Garance's spine. She imagines those buttons open, Garance reaching clumsily back there with her long pianist fingers to fasten them, calling for someone to help her in her partially unclothed state.

"You're going to be cold," is all Louise finds to say. "Don't you have a coat?"

"I'm much too excited to be cold! You're sure the dress is not too much?"

"I am telling you, you look very, very pretty tonight. But you are going to catch your death out there, you ridiculous coquette. Let me get you a shawl, at least."

As Louise grabs her black coat off the rack by the door, she also takes a heavy white wool shawl for Garance. It looks jarring, almost homely, against the glossy magnificence of the dress. Louise does not care: the girl must be shielded against the bite of the November night, as mild as she may think it is.

THE SKY IS BLACK, and the two women walk fast down the avenue de l'Opéra together. Louise lags back for a moment, letting Garance get a few steps ahead. She looks over the girl's upswept blond hair and her back, at the borrowed shawl slipping off her shoulders, her bare skin glowing white against the shocking red of her dress.

"Are you sure you're not cold in this getup?" Louise shouts after her.

"I'm telling you, I can't be cold this evening!" The girl laughs over

her shoulder without slowing her pace and without so much as looking at her teacher, who is hustling to catch up to her imperious stride.

It is a wonderful production. The sets are grandiose and lovingly
detailed. They sweep in and out of existence between scenes with
dizzying speed, on smooth and silent runners behind the heavy
velvet curtains. Carmen is a black-haired beauty with a small,
pursed red mouth and a profile that almost forms a straight line from
her forehead down to the tip of her nose. Her skin projects a golden
heat under the stage lights. They must have cast a genuine Spaniard
for the part. Her voice is rich and ringing, and she moves sinuously
through the story in a downright lewd way that transfixes the audi-
ence. When she throws the red flower to the fascinated Don José,
the slow arc of her arm is serpentine and suggestive.

> *L'amour est enfant de bohème,*
> *Il n'a jamais, jamais connu de loi.*[30]

   The children's chorus is a pack of well-choreographed, cherub-
faced boys who move in arabesques around the stage. They are all
wearing identical pink stockings. When Louise closes her eyes, she
can still see the little pink legs prancing about to their jaunty song,
Nous marchons la tête haute, comme des petits soldats.[31]

---

30. *Love is a gypsy child,*
     It has never, never known law.
31. *We march, heads held high, like little soldiers.*

Garance leans slightly forward in her seat during the entire show, her back erect in her corseted top. Louise sees the girl's chest heave during the last scene, her lower lip quiver at the swell of the music. Louise looks away toward the stage just in time to see Don José plunge his knife swiftly into Carmen's body. At the penetration of the blade into the chest, Louise starts, feeling that Garance's moist heated hand has suddenly found her own, gripping tightly. The girl is pressing her hand, squeezing for dear life, and a blast of liquid heat bursts through Louise's heart and up into her blood-flooded cheeks. She thinks the girl mustn't know what she's doing; she must be overwrought by the emotional climax of the production. She does not pull her hand away from Garance's warm grasp. She completely misses the final moment of the opera.

> *Ô ma Carmen, ma Carmen adorée!*
> *Arrêtez-moi, c'est moi qui l'ai tuée!*[32]

When Louise gets home, it is nearly midnight and her body is drained as if it has gone through some trial. Thinking that perhaps her husband is in bed already, she sidles into the apartment as quietly as she can, but when she hangs up her coat, she hears laughter coming from the kitchen.

Apparently Henri is still up, and he's brought Pierre home with him. They must not have heard her come in, because they don't greet her. She is about to announce herself but thinks better of it.

---

32. *Oh, my Carmen, my beloved Carmen!*
    Arrest me, it is I who killed her!

Instead, she sneaks through the darkened living room and stands off to the side of the open kitchen door, looking at the two men unawares. They are drinking white wine together and talking animatedly, their faces a high color from the alcohol.

Pierre has a dreamy look on his face when he says, "I swear, Henri, it was so magnificent that it transcended cocksucking. When I came into her mouth, she started to shiver and moan like she was coming too. I'd never seen anything like it. Like she was starving for it."

"You weren't touching her?" Henri queries. "You mean, she came just from sucking you off?"

"Yes! It was amazing. It was like worship. It's the sort of feeling people are always trying to get in church. The poor bastards, they're looking in the wrong place."

Louise smiles to herself in the shadows: this is what men talk about, when they're alone! She has caught them. It is good that the two of them hadn't invited her father along, because had she heard such words coming out of his mouth, she would have fainted immediately.

What should she do? She wants to burst into the room, giggling with naughty joy, and fling her clothes all over the place. She wants to receive instructions on how to administer transcendent fellatio. Oh, their shiny drunken eyes and their laughter—she wants to be part of it.

They would be so aghast if they knew she'd heard them. It would ruin their evening.

Gingerly, she tiptoes back into the entrance and opens the front door. This time, she does so theatrically, and clears her throat. She shuts the door loudly, and says, "Hello? Are you home?"

She hears the shuffle of chairs as the men rise to greet her. They look jolly as they step out of the kitchen and into the living room, certain that Louise had a sweet, innocent time at the opera and knows nothing of their male crudity.

"Ah, Louise," says Pierre, "good to see you. Henri says you're well, and he's right because you look lovely. How was *Carmen*?"

"Quite marvelous. The sets were beautiful."

"Yes, I heard it was a wonderful production. Well, I should be getting on now. I wouldn't want to keep the two of you from bed."

"Well, thank you for entertaining my husband."

"My pleasure."

They say good-bye warmly and drowsily, and as Henri walks his wife back to their bedroom, he holds her hand. Louise is delighted at the thrum of sex in her blood and wonders if her husband will make love to her tonight, or if he is too drunk. She mustn't get her hopes up; probably, he will go to sleep as soon as he lies down.

This thrum of sex, this slow unfurling of heat—there is something like possession about it, like the body being seized by an unchecked and dreadful force. The rush of blood from her frenetic heart is both exhilarating and ominous—like vertigo.

La Floride fleurie

—◦◦—

THE NEXT MORNING IS when Henri makes love to her—Saturday. She wakes up to a strange sound in her head: a constant note like the moan of the metro train echoing in the dark tunnel, or perhaps a dim, distant alarm. Her eyes pop open and the sound clears with a brief effervescent hiss. She backs up against her husband's warm slumbering body and discovers that he has an erection; she can feel it straining against her. She grinds against it. He wakes up.

They don't speak; their agreement is immediate—more urgent than it has been in a long time. He gathers her to him and kisses the back of her neck, begins to work the nightgown off her with his willful hands.

He turns her around and takes her face to face, the two of them moving slowly on their sides. His slide into her is easy. They are surprised and glad for this sudden passion. She sucks eagerly on his impatient kiss. She can taste on his tongue the cigarettes that he smoked last night with Pierre. She tries the best she can not to think of Xavier Langlais's face while her husband is inside her. She comes loudly, and several times, with a pained expression on her face that looks something like grief. Henri is not sure how to feel about her unusually expansive displays. He thinks he likes them. He wonders what brought them on.

THAT EVENING, LOUISE AND Henri Brunet sit across from Xavier and Pauline Langlais at a small rectangular table covered in white linen, in the fine (but not overly pretentious) restaurant Le Poquelin. It is named after the playwright better known as Molière. The establishment has a theatrical theme: burgundy velvet curtains and banquettes, etchings on the wall from productions of *Le Misanthrope* and *Le Bourgeois Gentilhomme*. The pictures depict men in wigs arguing with one another and women wearing heavy, voluminous dresses and fainting into chairs, one hand artfully arranged on their forehead—all those parted lips, in paroxysms of emotion, gasping at the edge of consciousness. Xavier comments that he likes the décor.

The owner himself serves them their first course: a house-made goose foie gras with wedges of toast, and four small salads. They share a bottle of red wine, except for Pauline Langlais, who has put one of her gloves in her wineglass in a touchingly dated ladylike gesture signifying that she will be abstaining from alcohol tonight. Louise was not aware that anyone still did this; such a thing is a remnant of the past century. It occurs to her that her own mother might have done this when she was pregnant with her brother.

This image pains her, and though she wants to let it slip away, she cannot, and asks Pauline directly, "Do you have a name picked out for the child?"

Henri looks at his wife with bewilderment, then glances at her still-full wineglass, perhaps wondering if she has been drinking more than she has let on. Pauline doesn't look surprised at this bold question, and answers placidly, "We were thinking of François if it's a boy, and Odile if it's a girl. We are hoping for a girl, this time. Boys are wonderful, but too many of them can run a mother ragged!"

"Well, to a girl, then," Louise toasts, and takes a sip of her wine.

The two men make eye contact across the table, as if asking each other how their wives have acquired such a level of intimacy.

"We had a good chat when we met the other day," Pauline explains to her husband.

"Ah, well, that is good," Xavier answers. "It seems we'll all get along famously as neighbors. How long have you lived in this building?"

"Since our marriage, nine years ago."

Louise hopes that they do not ask about children (the lack of children). It would be an indelicate question. Pauline might ask it, but certainly not the exquisitely polite Xavier, Xavier who dabs at his lips with his napkin in a slow and dreamy gesture, as if he is not entirely in the room.

His gaze is so curiously clear and blank, and Louise is inflamed by it: he is a hermetic man and she is dying to breach him. There is some hidden thing in him she wants to get to, and her desire to pull this thing from his flesh spins and flares in her like some spontaneously created sun, extant for no reason that she can fathom, but indestructible.

The conversation flows easily despite the febrile buzz rising in

Louise, and before long they are on their second course and their second bottle of wine. They are talking about travel. Xavier, before he married, was seized by wanderlust and spent time meandering in the United States before the war.

"It is a queer and primitive place," he says. "It is fascinating."

"How so, primitive?" Henri queries.

"I am thinking mostly of the state of Florida, that ill and gorgeous swamp. I was there . . . Well, I was trying to make money like a lot of young men. Land speculation, you see. There are alligators there bigger than a man, sunning themselves by the side of the road. They hardly fear us. They do not run away; they move only when they are hungry, and when they are hungry it is best for you to run away. I wager the armor of scales they have on their bodies could deflect a small-caliber bullet."

Louise imagines a bullet grazing the huge sinewy back, leaving the animal unharmed. She sees the triangular reptilian head turning slowly to investigate where the bothersome little impact came from—that yellow and hostile stare, unfeeling and cold-blooded.

"Oh, how dreadful!" she says, her voice alive with delight.

"You know what is most dreadful about that place is the climate," Xavier continues. "The heat and the humidity and the constant ruckus of thousands of disgusting insects—some cockroaches as big as the palm of the hand, Louise, and they fly. The first time I saw one was when I found it crawling in my cot. I screamed like a woman at the sight of it; it was shameful. Oh, that blasted animal-ridden heat—there were always glowing eyes at night. It was not possible to shine a light anywhere without it reflecting inside those eyes. I had bizarre nightmares about being trapped places and being watched—always this feeling of being watched by some vague malevolent sentience, as if Florida itself were alive. That jungle place. It gave me such night sweats."

Xavier is looking straight at Louise now, some wavering emotion blasting off him like heat off black asphalt in a tropical sun. "How thrilling and terrible that place must be," she says softly, looking back at him.

"You cannot imagine the lushness of the vegetation there, Louise. All this green and all these flowers, such bright and enormous flowers everywhere. They were lubricious and often shone with some viscous something, as if they were secreting some musk—and those yellow stamens heavily coated in pollen—oh, and those thick red petals as dark as blood, and some of them even had little curved sacs at the base. I'd never seen anything like those blooming obscenities. You cannot imagine an orchid in the wild, the plant winding through the brambles and that strange and evil flower hovering there. When you visit a hothouse, you have time to gird yourself for that wicked plant, but when you come upon it unexpectedly—what a shiver."

Everyone at the table has stopped eating. Louise is not even breathing. She is transfixed by the flushed face of the man speaking to her. Certainly he is speaking to her alone because his gaze is fixed on her.

"You make it sound like an ecstatic experience," she says.

"It was. It nearly wrecked my life. I was nearly eaten whole by that ghastly place and its fevers, you know. It is so fecund and so unkind, that florid Florida."

"Oh, Xavier, you are drunk," Pauline says good-naturedly.

"Orchids are comestible, you know," Xavier feels compelled to add. "They taste almost like nothing. Just fresh and moist, like an ocean breeze."

Louise turns and looks at her husband. He has an uncharacteristic tight and angry expression on face. There is something about the tense posture of his body that makes her think that he knows with all his soul that she is wilting with desire for this near stranger and his risqué stories about tropical vegetation. She suddenly visualizes him picking up his steak knife and lunging across the table for Xavier's throat. What a strange idea, her even-tempered husband!

Still, she sees this. She sees her husband plant the blade with a swift sweep of the arm into the side of the man's neck—the blade sticking there; the knife handle erect and grotesque in the new wound, just beginning to gush; the look of horrified surprise on Langlais's face, unable to let out a scream as his blood flows thickly onto his white shirt collar. Why does she see this?

Her husband looks cross, but this cannot be. It must be her fanciful brain getting away with itself. Really, nothing has happened. Everything is jovial. The plates are taken away. They order dessert. Henri wants nothing. Xavier orders a chocolate mousse that he shares with his wife. Louise is surprisingly hungry; she eats a whole wedge of apple tart by herself. The crust is warm and flaky. The apple slices fall apart sweetly on her tongue, and she sings the praises of this heavenly confection. She offers it to her husband to taste, but he insists that he cannot eat another bite.

She wants to offer a piece to Xavier. She wants to see him lean across the table to take a sweet directly from her fork, to engulf with his mouth a place where her lips have been. She restrains herself.

The check comes. Henri picks it up.

"Ah, no," Xavier says, "let me get that. Let me thank you for introducing us to this lovely eating place."

"I insist. Let me treat you."

"Absolutely not," Xavier maintains, opening his wallet and pulling out a few bills. "Really, dear Sir, it will be my privilege. Tonight I seem to have a little bit of stray cash yearning to be released."

As he says this, he is looking straight at Louise with a slightly crooked half smile on his face. With what slow relish he pronounces the words "stray cash"—what a terrible man.

Oh—he knows! Of course he knows that she is the naughty letter writer and he displays this knowledge by sliding her pun back at her across the table like so much paper money. That smirk of his: so lewd and so attractive. Louise is going to faint. She is going to cry. She is going to palm her breasts. She is going to reach blindly under the table for his stirring cock.

No, she will do nothing, of course. She is civilized. She will merely let her body hum with frustrated sex. He is playing with her, the bastard, and she flutters with abject happiness at this—at this drawing out of illicit desire while maintaining perfect deniability. She cannot stand this! It is too much. It is just enough. She is thrilled.

Henri shrugs as he gives up the check, taking his hands off the table. "As you wish, then. Thank you very much for this splendid dinner."

Xavier counts his money into the small silver tray, and asserts, "Certainly it is my pleasure, dear Sir."

11 Novembre

ON THE ELEVENTH HOUR of the eleventh day of the eleventh month in the year 1918, the fires cease.

ON THE ELEVENTH DAY of the eleventh month in the year 1923, the flame of the unknown soldier is lit at his tomb under the Arc de Triomphe. This light will always burn. On the day you read this record, the flame burns. On the morning of the eleventh day of the eleventh month in the year of our story, 1928 (Sunday), this flame burns. As Louise wakes up next to her still-sleeping husband, this flame burns. As she looks him over with great tenderness, this flame burns. As she goes about her business on this day of remembrance, the tenth anniversary of the Armistice, this flame burns.

LOUISE IS BESIDE HERSELF. She has no idea what will happen next. Clearly something is going to happen. This elates her and makes her angry at the same time. She watches her husband to see if he suspects. It seems that all is well with him as he sips his morning tea and reads the newspaper.

She is quite sure she cannot stand this. She will go mad.

As she sits there with her cooling tea in front of her, she hears music. It is a slight and wistful melody coming from the street. Louise gets up and opens the window.

"Look!" she says to her husband. "An organ-grinder."

He grunts an acknowledgment that she has spoken, but doesn't seem interested by this news. No matter. Louise looks down into the street at the fellow pushing his wheeled musical contraption. He is dressed in faded and patched clothing, and wears a cap tilted at a jaunty angle, along with fingerless gloves. He looks straight ahead as he turns the crank on his machine, rolling it down the street.

His song nudges at Louise's ear. Something about it makes sweat break onto the skin of her back. "I think I shall give him a few coins," she says.

"Very well," answers Henri.

She runs to fetch some spare change out of her coat pocket, then runs back to the open window. She flings her money into the street. It falls in a graceful, glimmering arc in the morning light and makes a small ringing shower when it hits the hard ground. The music stops as the musician bends over to pick up the coins. He puts them in a cup hanging off the side of his organ and looks up at Louise.

"Pretty melody!" she shouts down at him.

He touches his fingers to the brim of his cap and gives a small bow. He continues his progress down the street, resuming his song. As he turns the corner, Louise hears the resounding evidence of another donation being made from another window farther along.

Even after the music has faded into the distance, Louise is still humming the catchy and haunting tune. She goes into the piano room, the room where she gives Garance her lessons every week, and picks out the notes from the stranger's organ on her own instrument, with her wandering fingers.

She plays the song. She adds chords. She adds her own flourishes until the melody doesn't sound like itself anymore. It is a new creature, and Louise goes wherever it takes her. It is like an animal pulling on its leash, humoring her human need to have a grasp on it, but nevertheless able to bolt off and away whenever it chooses. It is not domesticated; it takes her up and down the register on the piano without her planning three notes ahead. It is an errant breed, and she follows it to its quiet, melancholy little death.

When she finishes playing, she notices that she is trembling. She looks up and sees her husband leaning against the frame of the doorway, observing her silently with both hands in his pockets.

"That was quite beautiful," he says, cocking his head at her.

"Then why do you look so puzzled?"

"Well, you hardly play like that anymore. I don't think I've heard you play for yourself like that in years, actually. What made you do that?"

"I . . . I'm not sure. I'm just feeling a bit restless today."

Henri laughs. "Well then, maybe you should go for a walk. I have a little bit of bookkeeping to do for the shop today anyway."

"Henri?"

"Yes?"

"Don't you miss me, sometimes?"

"What do you mean, Louise? You're not leaving, are you?"

His tone is not amused now. He looks concerned, and Louise feels guilty for rattling him. "Oh no, don't worry, darling. I will just go for a little walk, and be back in time to make us lunch."

"All right, then. Enjoy yourself," he says, and disappears from the open doorway, back to his work.

The melody is thus:

On her way out of the building to take her walk, Louise checks her mailbox on impulse. It is a silly thing to do: it is both a Sunday and a national holiday. Of course, there should be nothing. No government functionary is working today. It would be ridiculous to expect any letters.

Still, a lone envelope tumbles out into her hand when she opens the small squeaking metal door. It does not bear a stamp and is addressed only to *Madame Louise Brunet*. Clearly, whoever has sent this missive has dropped it into the slot directly, without the intervention of a postman. It must be an urgent message.

A burst of tingling warmth travels through her entire body and makes her vision dim for a moment. She has to brace herself against the wall. As she tears open the flap, her hands shake—have they stopped trembling since she played that strange little song on the piano?

There is only a single sheet inside the envelope. The handwriting, though quick and slanting, is perfectly legible:

---

33. Whose handwriting is this? Why does this exist? It cannot be part of the record.

Dear Madam,

Tomorrow—Monday—I will take a stroll on my lunch break in the Père Lachaise Cemetery. I will be at the southwest entrance that leads into the avenue Principale at a quarter to one sharp. You will be there also. You will be waiting for me. You will be ready for me.

As you can see, I have agreed to the expression of your most distinguished sentiments,

Sir

This is the most ghastly, the most thrilling thing she has ever read—his presumption! He knows who she is, and he has taken possession of her already. A man so brazen—it would serve him right for her not to go to this imperiously stated rendezvous. And what a lugubrious and perverted idea, to meet in a cemetery! Does he intend to enter her body in some broken, desecrated family crypt? What manner of business is this?

His panache is more than she can stand. He must be a perfect match for her. She does not know how she will prevent herself from spontaneously combusting over the course of the next day. She is convinced that flames will explode forth from her traitorous heart and her hysterical womb and consume her corrupted flesh entirely before the bastard can even lay a hand on her, secure in his ownership.

This is too much, too much to bear. She cannot wait.

On the eleventh hour of the eleventh day of the eleventh month in the year 1928, this flame burns.

Possession

SHE STANDS AT THE gate. She has made herself pretty for this encounter, painted her lips vivid red and put on her violet cloche hat. She forces herself to stand completely still, clutching her pocketbook with both hands. She will not be found pacing like an animal. She will not be seen to be anxious.

There he is, walking up the street toward the appointed place. For a moment his eyes slide over her, then make contact. Now they are fixed on her, and that half smile begins to play on his lips again. That mouth of his makes her want to scream; it smirks with hidden knowledge. For all his smugness, there may be something disarming about that lopsided expression, something like embarrassment, as if he were shy. She cannot be sure.

As he passes her, his shoulder brushes against hers. He stares straight ahead and continues walking, as if the touch were accidental. In that moment she sees the side of his face, sees the flash of a network of faintly exploded blood vessels just at the place where his left ear meets his cheek. His handsomeness seems enhanced rather than marred by the discovery of this small defect. She follows him, walks in step next to him. For several minutes, they wind their way through the streets of the cemetery without speaking. They take in this strange city of the departed with its cobblestones and its mausoleums, a walled-in, dead, miniature Paris ensconced within the live Paris. It's a romantic place, and couples must come here often to reflect on the glorious love affairs of all the rich and glittering people buried here.

Suddenly Xavier stops, and Louise stops with him. They are before a flat-topped grave, and she wonders with a shiver whether he intends to have her sit on the grainy stone, relieve her of her undergarments, and penetrate her in this place. It would make quite a story, if she could tell anybody. Perhaps a child would issue from such a moment (her heated body tells her the timing might be right for this) and perhaps the child would be a girl. The child and Louise would be close. They would share all their secrets. One day after the child is grown, Louise could tell her of this moment. What a revelation that would be, to learn that your father is not your father! Louise's heart feels a pinch of empathy for this nonexistent girl. She is dying for this girl to exist, possibly even more keenly than she is dying for the intrusion of this man's sex into her own.

Xavier makes no move to touch her and instead reaches into the breast pocket of his coat to pull out a small book—what is this? Is he taking out a Bible? Is he going to tell her she is impure, with no virtue, and that she mustn't do this and that she must go home and pray? Perhaps she has utterly dreamed all his oblique lewdness.

"I've been teaching my boys something interesting," he says, "a Flaubert text called *Salammbô*. It is mostly about the butchery of war, and it is about Oriental women too, though all women really. Flaubert wrote his mistress a letter on the subject of Oriental women; it's here in this book. I am thinking of sharing this letter with my students, you see. Academically, it's fascinating. Would you like to hear it?"

Is this his method of seduction? Louise leans against the grave and puts her hand on the granite slab to steady herself. It is faintly cool and moist, almost like earth. There is nothing to do but accept the moment. She nods, lets him read:

> The Oriental woman is a machine, and nothing more. To smoke, to go to the baths, to paint her eyelids and drink coffee, this is the circle of occupations where her existence revolves. And as for her physical pleasure, it must be quite light, because quite early in life, that famous button, the seat of her pleasure, is cut from her. And this is what makes her, this woman, so poetic from a certain point of view, it's that she reenters nature absolutely.
>
> I have seen dancers whose bodies swung with the rhythm of the unfeeling furor of a palm tree in the wind. This eye so full of depth, where there are dimensions colored like the sea, expresses nothing but calm, calm and emptiness, like the desert . . .
>
> From whence does the majesty of their form come? Perhaps from the absence of all passion.

With these words, Xavier shuts his book and puts it back inside his coat. He asks Louise, "What do you think? Do you think my students will find this interesting?"

He stands there without reaching for her, and she is quite sure she wants to wrap her hands around his neck and squeeze. What does the infernal bastard want from her? Is he saying that if she were some empty vessel, free of desire—then he would find her attractive? What manner of trap has he laid for her today? She feels she might collapse on the gravestone and cry, but a great resolve not to give him that pleasure grips her, since who knows, perhaps this is what he wants: simply to break her, to see emotion explode from her helpless heart the way the too-sweet flesh from a half-rotten fruit would burst forth into the hand when it is pressed too hard.

His hands are in his pockets. He stands there watching her placidly, completely shielded by his coat. She wants to leap on him and tear the clothes from him, get this over with—or perhaps kill him instead? In a fit, she might pick up a loose cobblestone and dash his brains all over the ground with it. It would certainly crown the strangeness of this unexpected day.

"Dear Sir," she says, her voice high with quivering wrath, "I too have a story that you might find of academic interest. Do you remember the piece of artillery they called the Paris Gun? This was toward the end of the war, and the Germans were shelling the city with it. Do you remember? It was the largest gun ever built and could shoot the farthest. It was many miles away from the city. Do you remember? The barrel of the thing often got so overheated that it would warp and then it had to be changed. The accuracy of the weapon was also quite poor. The Germans only succeeded in hitting the outskirts of Paris with it. This famed and enormous gun did not do much, though oceans of money were drained into it. Think of the size of the foiled investment. It was hardly used and hardly inflicted any casualties. Militarily, it was a failure. It could only hit city-sized targets and was not too successful at doing that. Do you remember?"

Xavier doesn't move when she tells him this, but she can see that she has affected him. His face is suddenly a florid red. His jaw ripples with a wave of tension. He must be puzzled and furious, and she is glad. Her voice thick with mockery and rage, she says with a creeping smile, "What a pity, no? Such a big gun, and such a failure."

Something electric travels up from the ground and shoots its way into Xavier's body. Louise can see it move through him like a wave. His back straightens and his eyes widen; he is galvanized. She thinks at this moment that he might press himself against her and push her back onto the grave and crawl in heated fury all over her—to take her, finally! She thinks that this must be the moment. She is convinced that she can see the impulses of his torsioned heart, his overwrought sex. Is she victorious?

"You wish to see failure?" Xavier growls from deep in his throat. "I will show you failure."

With these words, he turns on his heel and walks quickly away from Louise toward the gate of the cemetery, his steps echoing eerily on the cobblestones.

Louise's ride home on the metro passes through her in a blinding rage. She cannot even begin to believe the foolishness that just happened. She hates him so much! If she were a man, she would beat him senseless. She would take great joy in feeling his muscle give beneath her punches. His groans of pain would be music to her ears. If he fell beneath her assault, she wouldn't stop: she would kick him while he was down. She wonders if she could feel his ribs crack—would she be able to hear some sticklike snapping sound?

The blood from his broken nose streaming over his lovely mouth—oh—the lust in her body has curdled to violence like sweet milk spoiling to sourness. As if she smells this sourness, she wrinkles her nose and cringes in her seat. She is disgusted with him and with herself.

There is a man sitting in the seat across from her reading a newspaper, unsuspecting of the silent female storm within arm's reach. She wants to tear the newspaper from him and open her coat to display her body to him. She wants to ask this stranger: if this woman here were offered to you, would you refuse? Why would a man refuse if it's easy?

Why would a man signal that he is accepting, that he is ready to pluck the overripe fruit from the gnarled branch of the forbidden tree just as it is about to fall? Why would a man do that and then toss the fruit aside without even deigning to step on it as he walks away, to grind its corrupted flesh into the earth where it belongs?

This is funny, after all, all this useless comedy.

She turns her head and looks at herself reflected in the black glass of the train car. Her face is pale and set in an expression she herself cannot read. Her features feel heavy, almost monumental: it seems that even an effort of will cannot move them. She tries to understand whether what she is feeling is sadness or anger, but comes up unknowing. She decides that she will smile at herself, that a false expression is better than no expression at all.

She forces this smile, and it creeps across her numb red lips; it creeps across and stops. She is frozen for a moment in this willed rictus of contentment, and sees that her grin is small and lopsided.

It looks like Xavier Langlais's smirk. She is struck to the core by this similarity.

Ah, but she can see her wet eyes drowning in her dark reflection. She registers her own distress and looks elsewhere, turning away her rising feelings—her rising feelings always turned away. There is nothing to be done about this. This repression is as inexorable as the rot that turns the body of a beloved man into mulch for the scrubby grass on his grave.

A beloved man of her own blood, a beloved man hardly more than a boy. Taken by war, taken by sickness—what does it matter? Two bodies that grew strong tussling with each other in the backyard. Two pairs of ears arrested in the staircase by the call of her piano-playing, on the way to the kitchen to fill two stomachs with crusty bread and chocolate. Play it again, Louisette. That was pretty. Did you make that up?

Which one of them asked her to play it again?

What does it matter? They're both gone now. Dissolved into the earth.

She closes her eyes and listens. As the train plows through the tunnel, the tracks moan beneath it and reverberate all around. It is not an entirely unpleasant sound: all-encompassing and multitonal, but almost flutelike, almost beautiful.

One note rises above all the others in the echoing swirl of metal melody, and its mournful swoon sinks into Louise's body like the heat from a warm bath. It is an A-sharp.[34] As the train turns and

---

34. An A-sharp. Is this the pitch of the vibration in my body? A melancholy and lovely note.

the tracks grind, Louise hums along with this one note deep in her throat, as if responding to a musical greeting. The man across from her does not hear her since her hum matches the tone of the train so perfectly—her gentle release, completely undetected.

Possession, bis

~❧~

THAT AFTERNOON, XAVIER'S TEACHING is on fire. He reads Flaubert's letter about the Oriental woman to his boys. They are mesmerized. They stay completely silent because they don't want to break the stride of his words; they are afraid that should he pause, he will realize that the secrets he is giving them are utterly inappropriate (he even utters the word "orgasm" into their stunned and elated ears). They are afraid that should he pause, he will get flustered and stop.

They don't know that his momentum is too strong to be stopped by mere decency. They don't know that passion grips his brain like a disease and that he is helpless against it. They follow his dreamy gaze as he speaks about sex and the shuddering fevers of possession to see what he sees, but they see only out the window. They see only the image of the Paris skyline cut cleanly against the blank gray sky. The sun is not to be seen anywhere through this soft haze, which is to be expected in November—though this November is strangely warm despite the dimness of the light. Despite the dimness of the light, sweat sticks a man's shirt to his back should he walk too fast, or talk too fast, or get overly excited.

Xavier's face is flushed and gleaming with perspiration. As helplessly as his flustered pores pour forth sweat, his mouth pours forth lectures about women, about mysterious fires in the blood; he cannot help himself. Still, he is happy at this moment. He can tell that his students are listening, truly listening to him today as he tells them, "They are aching for it too, you know, perhaps as much as we are. What if it's more, can you imagine? You never know what manner of sensuous and exquisite hell is roiling in those bodies of theirs. Their bodies do not signal arousal as crassly as our bodies, the infernal creatures. But sometimes you will see them boil forth— you will see them boil forth with impersonal and all-destroying desire and you will be stunned and you will be conquered and how prone we all are to such sickness!"

He interrupts himself, and looks over the room full of adolescent faces raptly turned toward him. He glances at the watch that he plucks from his pocket. The bell will ring soon, and the realization of what he has said to them for the past hour washes warmly over him. But he is not embarrassed and he is not frightened; he is conspiratorial. He says to them, "Now pack up your books and go home, and think on this. This new disease that you have in your blood now, boys, it will never get better. But, they have the same disease. We all manifest it in our ways. What I have just told you, dear boys, don't tell a soul. You wouldn't want to get a giving teacher such as myself in trouble, would you?"

For several seconds, an electric silence, and then the boldest boy says aloud, with military gusto, "No, Sir!"

They all laugh, and Xavier shuts his tiny book with a swift snap of his hand, tucks it back into his breast pocket.

———

THIS DAY (MONDAY) XAVIER Langlais feels exceedingly peculiar. As a matter of fact, he feels so peculiar that he is half-convinced that he is somehow outside himself. Or no, rather, he is inside himself, but someone or something else is inside his body too, turning up the heat. On his ride home on the metro, his brain crackles with the memory of his strange lunchtime rendezvous, with the extraordinary session he has given his students, with this other vaporous presence superimposed on his flesh, directing him. He is filled with his own surging pulse. His sweat output has not gone down but increased. He shivers. Is he afflicted with some sort of fever? He cannot tell for certain what is happening to him. He shifts in his seat. He jiggles his foot. His back is sore.

That confounded woman. His confounded self. At this moment, he is filled with dark need, and he wonders why exactly he feels so uncivilized, so uncontrolled. It must be that damned Louise has infected him! Or resuscitated him. His long-lost fighter pilot the Angle must be preparing for a mission of some sort, because Xavier's head is spinning. He feels that he might fall on his knees and vomit, right here in the train car, spraying his stomach juices across the aisle.

Something in him keeps his back straight, keeps him from losing control of his swooning body. A great burst of heat tingles in his solar plexus. It floods his musculature to his fingertips, seeps into his bones. The feeling is pleasant. It agrees with his body. Arousal stirs, and he must rest his briefcase on his lap.

Surely such a surge of unexplained emotion will bring about disaster: this illness—this feeling of falling—the engines roar and his eyes are tingling with smoke. He must disengage his flying machine. He must pull up but he cannot.

His body braces itself for the crash because all of Xavier Langlais is on the same wavelength now; all of Xavier Langlais is suddenly abloom with maleness. He knows now what he will do. He will emerge from the metro, breathing in the moist heavy air aboveground, breathing in the weak light of the impending winter. He will walk home across the Palais Royal garden at a brisk pace, undoing his tie and popping open the first two buttons of his shirt to get a breeze to his flushed skin.

He will get to his building. He will enter. He will go up the stairs. He will quietly bypass the door to his own apartment, the door behind which his wife and his sons wait idly for him, secure in the knowledge that he will be there shortly. He will go one floor up. He is fairly sure that Louise will be alone, because her husband works later than he does. He knows he will do this. He already has a story ready for his wife to explain his delay. He will say that the metro broke down and he had to wait for a whole hour for the train to start up again, trapped in the tunnel dark and wishing only to go home.

He is neither happy nor sad over his impending marital betrayal and his clever, ready little lie. He is driven by something he cannot understand—some unknown thing inside him pushes him on and he yields. It must be that whatever is to follow is already written.

Paris

May 13th

Dear Sir,

Early this morning, on the birthday of the dead woman who has been haunting me, I fold a hand-painted white silk handkerchief into my breast pocket. I check an address on a calling card, this one:

I find this address on my map. I am going to go. I am going to find out what is really there, now. Today—happy birthday, Louise. Down into the metro I go, with the card tucked behind the handkerchief in my breast pocket, next to my beating heart.

The squeals of the train in the tunnel sound almost melodious today. I hum along with them as I would a song. The stop I am going to is called Pyramides. When I emerge back above ground, I can see the opera house down the avenue. I immediately find the street I am looking for, and it is bizarre how quickly the noise from the avenue fades away once I get to number 13. I pause in front of a red door, its paint peeling and revealing previous layers of color: black, green. I have to go in. It's too late now to turn back.

The entryway is chilly, and to my right is a hive of mailboxes. Someone is playing the piano in one of the upper stories; the music echoes down the courtyard. The melody sounds quite familiar, but I cannot place it—then I notice the small metal placard on one of the mailboxes, the type set white on navy blue, in all capitals.

LANGLAIS

the type spells,
and for a moment I am quite certain that I am going to run out of
the building, screaming.[35]

Everything is just like what I have seen in my waking dreams. A man issues from the staircase, a fellow with dark receding hair carrying a caramel-colored satchel, presumably heading to work. He is wearing a high rounded collar such as were popular during the 1920s. He smiles at me as he passes as if he knows me, a crooked half smile that shows off his startlingly beautiful mouth, ripe with pinkness.

---

35. The melody—oh, the melody. I do not know music, but I am quite certain it is this:

Help me!

Stunned, I turn to watch him go. I follow him into the street, but he pays me no attention. I want to shout after him, but I notice the street is different from before. The parked cars have disappeared. The storefronts are different, and the few people walking there are dressed like—

Oh, it is so much colder than mere seconds ago, like a November morning.

I shout, "Xavier!" but he does not turn around, as if he doesn't hear me. Or perhaps that is not his name after all. I turn to look at the door I have just exited, and it is green, freshly painted. I am going to faint. But not in the street. I scramble back inside the building, where the piano music has stopped. The mailboxes are now on the left, and not a single one is labeled Langlais, or Brunet. The front door is once again red, peeling. Oh, but there is a familiar name on one of the mailboxes: the inhabitant of the third floor is named Josianne Noireau.

Her! Of course I knew she had something to do with this. Without a moment's thought, I burst onto the staircase and run up to her front door, across a landing that is tiled in stark black and white, like a chessboard. I lean on the doorbell for several seconds, its shrill alarmed sound a perfect reflection of the feeling in my overwrought body. I am determined to have an explanation from her. The door opens, and there she is looking up at me, all disordered red hair and amusement. She is wearing a diaphanous white nightgown that lets me see the outline of her body—a fine body indeed, and once again I am disarmed.

"You live here," I sputter.

"I do. Would you like some tea? I was just making myself some breakfast. I'm delighted to see you."

That confounded woman! Was she expecting me?

Sitting across the kitchen table from her, across steaming cups of tea, I cannot keep my eyes off her. She has not bothered to put on a robe to cover herself. She must see me looking. I am no master of slyness.

"Vous avez quelque chose à me montrer, Trevor?"[36] she says, her voice soft and slightly raspy, as one who had just gotten up. As my answer, I take the handkerchief out of my breast pocket and lay it gently on the table before her, like so:

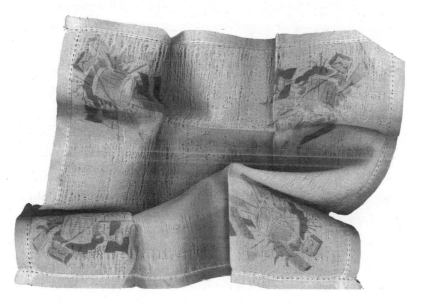

"Ah," she says.

"Well? Do you know when it is from? From which war?"

___

36. "You have something to show me, Trevor?"

"None of us have ever figured that out."

"None of you? Not even the historian? How many of us have you collected?"

"Oh, not that many, Trevor. Don't be jealous."

She seems genuinely worried that I'm angry now, and I am flustered. That is not after all what I want her to think of me. I want to reassure her, but the only words that suddenly pop into my whirring brain are *I love you*. Foolishness! Complete foolishness. I do not speak.

"How are the fevers?" she asks.

"They do not abate."

She lays her cool white hand on my cheek. It feels quite soothing there. "Are they very bad? That would be terrible. Are you not enjoying your research?"

"Oh, I am. It's been a fine journey, I assure you."

"I did want you to enjoy it, Trevor."

I take her hand and cup it in my own; I kiss the underside of her delicate wrist, just at the juncture with the palm, such a sensitive and ticklish place. She titters, and I wonder, Would her hands fit into Louise Brunet's mesh gloves? What a dreadful thought, to slip such lovely, live flesh into the garments of ghosts! But have I not been slipped thus inside the record?

"When you drop a handkerchief in front of somebody," I ask, "is that not a gesture of courtship?"

"Yes, but usually it is the woman who does it."

"Well, you did, didn't you? You dropped it first."

She comes around the table and slides herself onto my lap. She wiggles as she settles there. My nose nearly touches her neck; I can smell the fragrant heat of her hair. She is a terrible, mischievous woman who has played me an enormous trick, and I am quite sure I am in love with her. I encircle her waist with my arms and I can feel through the thin cloth what my eyes suspected: she wears nothing under the nightgown. The fit of our bodies is perfect; it is as if it was meant to be.

"I suspect we are not going in to work today," I whisper into her ear.

For a reply, she kisses me on the mouth and all is forgotten and all is remembered and it is as if I have no volition as I yield to this desire—and I have never been so happy. Oh, darling, tell me you will look at me like this again tomorrow! Tell me you will remember these kisses, that they really happened. Don't wave me off, those fathomless gold-flecked eyes closed to me, and say, "Non, non—pas encore . . ." *Encore, s'il te plaît, encore!*

Oh, Sir, I forget myself! I apologize. Findings:

1. a photograph.
2. an empty envelope.
3. coins.

I hope life is treating you as well as it is treating me. I suspect so.

Sincerely,

Trevor Stratton

Trevor Stratton

De garde dans les tranchées

In the documentation, another soldier stands his weary guard:

En Lorraine : de garde dans les tranchées.

His face looks familiar to you. You have seen him before. You cannot be certain where because faces have been recurring around you in a strange way lately. For all you know, you might have gazed into that man's eyes a week ago on the street. You wonder whether the soldier's pants are red or khaki. France started the war dressed in red pants and blue coats, but the red pants turned out to be so visible that they were practically bullet beacons. It was a strange war; war had to be learned all over again. It was the bloody birth of the twentieth century.

You swear you have seen this man's face before, with his coat buttoned all the way up like that, against the cold he suffers from—artfully arranged and still for a moment—the moment of picture-taking. Ah, yes, there we are:

First row, first Frenchman all the way on the left, feet crossed right over left, same distant facial expression. This fellow *in Lorraine: on guard in the trenches,* as he has helpfully written in violet pencil on the bottom of the first picture, is also on the postcard Louise's father sends home on October 12, 1918. Who is this fellow? And why is Louise's father not in the collective photo?

It comes to you all at once; it comes to you like the blast of a nearby shell that knocks you clean down but somehow leaves you uninjured, yet makes you deaf in your left ear (the other ear works just fine). This man is Pierre Cleper. He was at the war with

Louise's father, in the same company. Louise's father was the only one who knew how to properly work the camera, how to properly immortalize Pierre Cleper in the trench, posed surrounded by his accoutrements. His own gaze, properly immortalized: Pierre Cleper is looking back at him—

Pierre Cleper is looking back at you

through the lens.

All of them are looking at you, all of them properly immortalized for the record, captured by unseen eyes:

huddled together, but strong

still for a scrap of time

for this picture

look at it

they want you to.

[NB: An empty envelope, addressed to Monsieur Camille Victor, 3rd Battalion, 2nd Company, 1st Section, Postal Sector 68. Stamped in violet ink: The addressee could not be reached. RETURN TO SENDER. The date mark is too blurry; you cannot read when the letter was returned. The letter came back to Louise the day before she got word from her aunt, Camille's mother, that she had received the telegram. She did not need word of the telegram. The returned letter was enough. She tore it open with trembling hands and read over her last words to Camille, words that never reached him. She ripped this letter to tiny shreds and threw it away. She erased it from the record. Yet she stayed her hand when she was about to dispose of the envelope. Somehow she wanted to preserve it, that empty remnant of the seemingly endless weeping that would rack her body for days.]

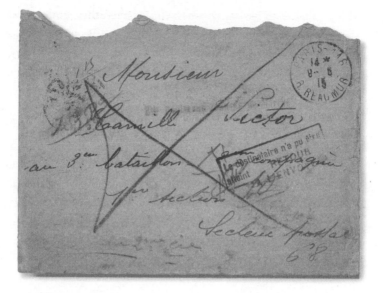

[NB: Shot on the battlefield like so many others. There is no way to know where in the body, how many times, and how long it took him to die. Half a heartbeat, hours, days? It is possible that death was kind. Perhaps the bullet struck him in the head, penetrating the bone with disconcerting ease. Perhaps his cranial plate shattered from the impact, a little. Perhaps he did not have time to suffer, did not have time even to formulate the thought that he was dying. We can pray that it was so.

Perhaps death was slightly less kind. Perhaps the bullet tore through his throat, making a neat hole through his trachea, the air sucked clean out of him in the most painful second of his life. Perhaps he had time to lie there for a few minutes, unable to scream, as he drowned in the blood from his wound. We can pray.

Perhaps death was very unkind. Perhaps he was shot in the back, the bullet hitting him right at the base of the spine, a little to the right—just where the padded flesh of his buttock tapered to an end.

The bullet shredded its way through the springy muscle tissue at his waistline, then tore its way through his viscera like so much tissue paper. The bullet fell not far from his feet, slickly covered in his blood, but he didn't see it. He was too busy being aghast at the gaping hole in his gut, from which his entrails were beginning to spill. It hurt so much that he had no idea what to do with himself except scream like he had never screamed before, knowing he was condemned to lie there for hours, maybe days, as he was taken by internal hemorrhage, or sepsis, his poisoned blood slowly seeping. His body fighting to live—this was what drew it out. This was the worst thing of all. He could not reach his gun to quicken his death—or perhaps he did not have the courage. Perhaps he hoped to the last moment that someone would come for him and save him. Perhaps he curled up into the mire and howled Louise's name, and wept like a child. We can pray that it was not so.

Yet you can see him falling to his knees, pressing down on his gushing wound with the flats of both helpless hands. Yet you can see his blood spurting from his innards—all over his clothes—in his agony he topples. What will he do next?

With his stricken thousand-yard eyes, he will look up at you, standing there holding an empty yellowed envelope in your hand, an envelope addressed to him but canceled, and returned to sender. He will not know the envelope is empty. He will not even question what you are doing here, a ghostly apparition wearing strange clothes and looking awfully clean and serene for a man standing in the middle of a battlefield. The roaring of guns cannot reach you. The two of you inhabit an in-between silence. He will make a great effort to speak to you, to say simply, "That letter is for me."

"Yes."

"Read it to me."

You will, of course, not have the heart to tell him that the envelope is empty and that the letter is lost; it is not in the documentation. You will not have the heart to tell him that perhaps Louise destroyed the letter because it read:

> My Dear Beloved Camille,
>   I cannot go against the wishes of my father. We cannot marry. I am sorry. I will always love you. You must know that.
>   Louise Victor

You will not have the heart to tell him that such a message was the last thing she said to him. She herself could not even bear such an idea and had to annihilate its very existence. It made her pain so much worse. But you will not worsen his pain at such a moment.

He will close his eyes to listen to you read, and you will be kind to him. You will be kind and read a nonexistent letter. After all, you have written a love letter to a complete stranger before:

> My Dear Beloved Camille,
>   When will you come home to me? I miss you so. But we must not be mournful. We must look forward to the moment when my door will open and you will be standing there. You will take me in your arms and kiss me—oh, Camille, do you remember on the bed how my lips parted for you, darling? Next time I see you, they will again. Next time I see you, you must make love to me immediately. All this waiting is ridiculous.
>   You will be weary and broken, I know it. You men always try to be strong, but after you've seen what you've seen, it is not possible to not be broken. It's all right, darling, you can be vulnerable with me. After we marry I will mend you. You will have a lifetime to suck the nectar from my body and be heartened by its sweetness. I will

give you many children and we will spend many nights warmed by laughter and song. You know this, don't you? I do.

We will meet soon. You must never forget: you are the jewel of my life.

Love always,

Louise Victor

When Camille hears this, he will smile through his pain. He will smile through his pain and faint away before your watery eyes, his wan face resting on the ground as if on a pillow, his hands lax around his wound with the blood still flowing out of it. You can hope that death will take him before he wakes up again. You can hope that his suffering is at an end. You can pray.]

Espèces errantes

WITHIN THE BOX, NESTLED within the documentation, there is another, smaller box. This one can fit in the palm of your hand. It is rectangular and black, with a fading pattern of little blue birds and flowers. This is the lid on the box:

Would you like to open it?

Inside you find a bit of change, scattered on the cloth lining like so much stray cash. Why not drop the coins one by one along the way and see where we wind up?

This one is so light it feels like nothing, and quite dented, though it was in circulation only briefly. It is to be expected, after all, at a time when metal was so short. The coin was struck in the year 1944, and expresses values different from the usual LIBERTE•EGALITE•FRATERNITE. This one advocates TRAVAIL•FAMILLE•PATRIE, which are safer things to aspire to for a populace under the boot of an occupant. The man who died with this coin in his pocket cared only about the first two; over the course of his life, he had become utterly exhausted with the third.

Louise found the coin when she was folding up her father's clothes to give them away a few months after he had died. It made a sonorous ping when it dropped on the floor, out of the pocket of his gray suit jacket. The sound startled her, and when she found its source she slipped it into her own pocket and decided to keep it. After all, the Americans had just landed on the beach in Normandy, so perhaps the currency would look different in a few months. Perhaps this little occupation artifact would become something like a collector's item.

He had died with half a franc in his pocket, change from buying a cup of chicory in a bistro only an hour before his fatal heart attack. Soon the Germans would be gone and there would be real coffee again. If only he'd lived another year to be granted that last flicker of happiness.

Another half franc, this one heavier and in better shape, struck in better times: in the year 1922. The values displayed on this coin are reflective of the decade's economic drive: COMMERCE•INDUSTRIE. Why were Liberty, Equality, and Fraternity so neglected? It seems un-French.

The coin slipped out of another pocket on a surprising day in the late spring of 1922. This day a new student had come to Louise, a nine-year-old girl who told her straight out that she had grown bored with her previous piano teacher. She was named Garance Saccard and had eyes as green as a tender young plant. Her fine hair unraveled from her braid as if faintly electrified, and her fingers were long and narrow, strangely unchildlike. She utterly astonished Louise with her ease at the piano, as if she and the instrument were two animals that had a symbiotic relationship with each other. She and music were of one will.

Louise was happy that day: it was such a rare pleasure to have a pupil who understood her instructions so immediately, and who pulled music seemingly whole out of the thrumming piano, with no pain and no labor. She could see right away that the child possessed the sort of talent that could take her to a conservatory if she was so inclined. Louise hoped the child was so inclined, and would not become bored with her new instructor.

After Garance had left, Louise found a half-franc coin at the foot of the piano stool. Probably the girl's candy money had dropped out of her pocket while she played. It would have been kind of Louise to give the money back, but she kept it instead, to mark this day and the appearance of this startling young girl with a mischievous smile into her own slow, dull life. She still had many students at that time, to save up money for the financial burden of all the children she still thought she might have with Henri—her faith in this eventuality was just beginning to waver.

This worn coin displays more of the characteristics you are used to in French currency. It declares itself struck by the French Republic and features the icon Marianne. The other side proclaims LIBERTE•EGALITE•FRATERNITE, as it ought to. You squint at this coin in order to make out its denomination and the year it was struck. It has been so smoothed by time and handling that you can make out this information only when you hold it under a loupe. Even then, you cannot be entirely certain that you are reading it right. Nevertheless, you think you can see 10 centimes. You think you can read 1871.

We are reaching back into the prehistory of this record. This coin is twenty-five years older than Louise. Who else is twenty-five years older than Louise? Her father is.

This coin was in the pocket of his own father the day he was born. After pacing his house all day listening to his wife scream behind closed doors, he was granted the gift of a healthy boy. When his sister came out of the bedroom to tell him that all was over and all was well, he was so happy that he flung his arms out to hug her, swiftly freeing his hands, which had been tensely thrust down into his pockets. This gesture violently hurled this coin out of his pants. The clear, loud impact of it against the tile floor of the entryway startled them both so much that they gasped together, then laughed at themselves. The new father decided that he liked

the bell-like ping of the brand-new shiny
coin to announce the birth of his son;
he decided to keep it to remind himself
of this moment. (This moment: bittersweet
after all, since the Prussians
had just marched into Paris.)

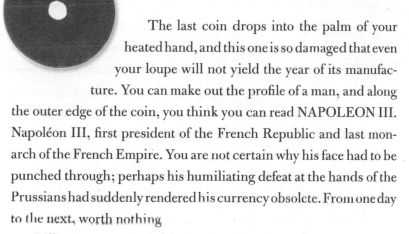

The last coin drops into the palm of your
heated hand, and this one is so damaged that even
your loupe will not yield the year of its manufac-
ture. You can make out the profile of a man, and along
the outer edge of the coin, you think you can read NAPOLEON III.
Napoléon III, first president of the French Republic and last mon-
arch of the French Empire. You are not certain why his face had to be
punched through; perhaps his humiliating defeat at the hands of the
Prussians had suddenly rendered his currency obsolete. From one day
to the next, worth nothing.

Still, someone saved this destroyed bit of stray cash to memo-
rialize something. Likely, it was Louise's grandfather. But here we
have attempted to reach too far back and we cannot see the day on
which this coin presumably dropped out of some pocket or other.
Before the birth of Louise's father, there is only a blank space; there
is only a darkness that even the boldest speculation cannot penetrate. Even the pluckiest falsifier cannot reach this time; he finds
himself dragged back across the years kicking and screaming,
leaving scratch marks back into the twentieth century, struggling
back across the hot coals of the Great War, gasping for air back
across the salty torrent of tears poured forth over a dead brother

and a dead lover, back through the dizzying years to the year of our story—oh it's so dizzying that you have to close your eyes and when you open them again, it is the afternoon of November 12, 1928, and Xavier Langlais has just rung Louise Brunet's doorbell, leaning on it with great gusto as if he has something very important to tell her. When Louise opens the door, she does not look at all surprised to see him there. She merely steps aside and lets him in. When she shuts the door, it takes a moment for her eyes to adjust to the dimness of the entryway. She looks up into his face. She isn't sure how to start. Apparently neither is he, since he is not moving, despite the glimmers of flame in his eyes.

"Haven't you done this before?" she asks him, without mockery.

"Done what?"

"Taken a woman not your wife. You looked to me like you had done this before."

He smiles at this, at this sudden softness. It's as if all their fury from earlier has evaporated, and now they are utterly flummoxed. They don't know what to do with themselves at this moment, at this genuine moment after all their posturing and violent ambivalence. Yielding disarms them, makes them into a couple of confused children, alarmed and elated at the vertiginous slide that awaits them. The tension in this pause makes them both unable to breathe, until Louise lets her body lean into his and suddenly his mouth—*Our Father who art in heaven,* his beautiful mouth!—is on hers. The shock of his tongue sends a shiver of electricity down her back; she wraps her arms around his neck, and he presses her against him. Their pulses speed. Louise pulls away when she starts to get dizzy. "I'm frightened," she whispers, "aren't you?"

"Of what?" he answers softly.

She laughs, with no rancor. "You—willfully obtuse! Answering questions with other questions!"

"Don't be frightened," he says. "It's easy. I promise. Even the lying is easy."

"Oh—I know."

He kisses her again. Already in a state of swooning arousal, Louise staggers back down the entryway; they take a few steps that way, their lips still connected. When they break apart, she takes his hand and leads him to the bedroom. They stand at the foot of the bed for a moment, close together, as if they are considering once more what they are about to do. Without saying a word, Xavier pushes her back until she falls on the bed with him on top of her—with his strong, warm body on top of her. She can feel he is hard for her oh—*forgive us our trespasses as we forgive those who trespass against us*—the pure unrestrained joy of it . . .

He begins to nibble the side of her neck; she starts to squirm, letting out something that sounds like a little hiccup when she feels his teeth—

hallowed be Thy name Thy kingdom come Thy will be done—

"Don't worry," he whispers into her ear, "I won't bite—hard."

She is practically sobbing with happiness when she reminds him, "Oh, make sure not to . . . oh, Xavier . . . make sure not to leave any . . . marks . . ."

He hikes up her blouse and pins her down on the mattress by the wrists, and she begins to shiver uncontrollably as he kisses and nibbles her stomach and breasts. When he moves her brassiere aside to suck her nipple into his mouth, she gasps. "Ah . . . please. Oh, please, Xavier . . . please."

lead us not into temptation but deliver us from evil—
Later Louise will wonder why it occurred to her to say that word (please); she never had in that context before. Yet today it seems fitting, and as he works her out of her clothes inch by inch, it keeps springing to her lips like a refrain. Once or twice it makes Xavier smile.

deliver us—

When he finally penetrates her, she says thank you.

Amen.

Dieu rit

—❧—

THE NEXT MORNING, LOUISE stays in bed while Henri gets dressed and makes himself a cup of tea. Through the haze of her half sleep, she hears him walk around the apartment. Then she hears an unlikely sound: the doorbell. Who could it be at this hour?

She listens to Henri's steps, the creak of the front door opening, voices. A young woman's voice. It sounds like—

This is strange.

Henri's steps again. He pops his head into the bedroom. "It's Garance. She wants to see you. She looks wound up about something. I'm going to work now, but you'll have to tell me what she wanted from you tonight."

"She didn't tell you?"

"No. She seems frightened of me. Maybe it's something woman-related."

Louise shrugs. "Don't know about that. Have a good day at work, dear."

"See you tonight," Henri answers, and leaves.

Still gummy-eyed from a night filled with bizarre and distressing dreams, Louise slips out of bed and pads her way to the living room in her nightgown, without so much as putting on a pair of slippers.

Garance is sitting on the couch in an uncharacteristically subdued way: slightly hunched over, with her schoolbag gathered on her lap, looking as if she is ready to make a quick dash.

"Good morning, Garance," Louise says. "Would you like some tea?"

The girl shakes her head no.

"What's the matter? What is this shyness? Shouldn't you be on your way to school right now?"

"I won't be long," says the girl softly. "I just came to give you a gift."

"What for? It's not my birthday."

"It's something I made for you."

Louise is both intrigued and unnerved by this irregular display. She goes and sits next to Garance, close enough so that their bodies are almost touching. The girl opens her bag and pulls out a small red notebook. She presents it to Louise, who takes it with a tentative smile. When she opens it and pages through it, she sees that it is entirely filled with sheet music, handwritten by Garance herself, the lines the notes rest on drawn in with a ruler.

"Garance, did you . . . Did you compose all these?"

"Yes. I wrote them all for you. I thought you should have them."

"But . . . but why?"

As Louise looks at the girl's face, at her shining eyes, she is suddenly conscious of the flimsiness of her nightgown and the soles of her bare feet being tickled by the carpet. Something odd is going on here. This has to be one of the queerest weeks that Louise has had in recent memory.

"I love you, Louise. I wrote these because I love you. I don't need to keep them because I have all the melodies memorized. It would make me happy for you to have them. To play them, even, Louise."

"Oh, I love you too, Garance. You're like a daughter to me."

"No, I'm not. I don't love you like that. I love you like music."

Ah, the girl had to go and say it. Louise's last attempt at willful obtuseness falls before Garance's relentless drive to speak her heart. Louise's hands begin to shake as they clasp her precious and unsettling gift.

"Garance, you are just confused. You love the music that I teach you. I see your passion for it, and you think that I am a vessel for your passion, but this thing that you feel, it is not a thing of the body."

At this pronouncement, Garance laughs, and before Louise can be offended at having her sage advice dismissed so swiftly by a mere child, the girl drops her bag to the floor and seizes Louise in her arms. The girl's fierce embrace will admit no refusal. Louise feels Garance's hands, still cold from her walk in the fresh, dim morning outside, against her warm and drowsy back. The girl's face is nestled in the side of her neck, in her loose hair. The girl says with great emotion, "I can feel your skin, Louise, through your nightgown."

Louise reaches around and rubs the girl's shoulders, in a gesture of comfort. The side of her neck, though it is warmed by the girl's breath, is ashiver with goose bumps. "My dear, please. It is not a thing of the body," she repeats.

The girl quivers at this, and Louise cannot tell now whether Garance is laughing or weeping. She is about to reassure the trembling child that all will be well when the trembling child pulls her face out of Louise's neck and presses her lips fiercely against her teacher's mouth.

For a moment, Louise is so startled that she does not move. She even has the fleeting thought that the kiss is not unpleasant, the soft curve of the girl's jaw so unlike a man's.

It is this thought that makes her pull back and scramble away, standing up so quickly that the little red notebook falls from her lap and lands at her feet with a decisive thwap.

"Garance!" she says, angry now, angry that she has come down to see this girl in her nightgown without so much as shielding herself in a robe first. The additional layer of cloth on her over-wrought body would have been a great help. Her body has been through entirely too much over the course of the past day!

"Oh, do you not love me anymore?"

"Of course I love you. Now please go to school."

The girl closes her book bag but makes no move to stand up. Her face is flushed and she looks about to cry.

"Darling, please," Louise says, gently now. "It'll be all right and you will get over this, this thing. It's not really from your body, my dear. It's from your music."

"Don't you see, Louise? It's the same thing. Music is a thing from the flesh. It's all the same. If you make me make music, then you're in my blood."

Louise feels like she might faint. This whole business is too much. Why did the girl choose today? Today is not the time. Not that any time is right for such absurdity, but today especially is not the time—not after Xavier.

Louise stands as straight as she can manage, attempting military authority with her posture, attempting to shield the warm storm of bewildered femaleness that rips through her entire self. She enunciates clearly when she gives her order. "Garance, go to school immediately."

The girl stands and picks up her bag, her mouth mellowing into a weak smile. "Am I coming back for my lesson tomorrow?" she asks.

"If you wish."

Garance nods, shoulders her bag, and leaves quietly. The two of them have accepted this moment. The moment has passed. It is already something else. They have already forgotten.

THAT CONFOUNDED GIRL!

With Garance gone, Louise looks over her gift. On the last page of the notebook, the written music interrupts itself, the melody merely stopped midsentence. There is no ending flourish, no crescendo. The line simply breaks. In the last corner of the last page, the girl has written her teacher a note:

> I have copied some of
> the best ones for you. I
> think they belong to
> you a little too. You can
> play them if you want.

With love, Garance

Louise loves her gift. She loves this music. She loves the girl so much that she could cry and she loves Xavier and she loves Henri

217

and she loves Camille and nothing makes any sense and her heart is exploded like so much shrapnel—she can feel gory pieces of emotion rising into her throat, constricting her breathing, taking her, irrepressibly. The first sob is wrenched from her with a great gush of hot tears.

[NB: This is a negative image of a document that does not exist.]

Louise is in the church again, the great hulking Gothic beast. This time she has to wait for her confession. While she does so, she crosses herself with holy water from the small marble basin at the entrance, white and filled with purity. She does so in the name of the Father, and of the Son, and of the Holy Spirit. Today she forgets to put her wedding ring on her right hand; she neglects this gesture of carnival. She is merely herself, going so far as to forget the mere possibility of subterfuge.

She kneels in the humid dimness of the wooden booth and closes her eyes. Suddenly she wants to laugh—she is trembling—she says in a quavering voice, "Bless me, Father, for I have sinned. It has been two weeks since my last confession."

"I am listening, my child."

"Yesterday I consummated a sexual union with a man to whom I am not married. It's terrible, you see: I am married to a man, but not this one. He is married too. He has children. I wish I had children. He is the most handsome man I've ever seen, and he is witty and strange and I am quite sure that I love him. When he came into me, it was as if the whole world tore apart and gave me a glimpse of something beautiful and it terrified me more than anything but I don't understand because I am quite sure I love my husband also but I am quite sure I want this man inside me again though the thought of his touch gives me vertigo. Father, the thought of his touch makes me feel like I am falling in the dark, forever. Father, I am not even sure that I have defiled anything. I am not even sure that I feel guilt. Is dizziness guilt? And then there is that confounded girl—Father, is it unnatural for a woman to love a woman as a man loves a woman? It does not feel unnatural, but it feels utterly incorrect, and sometimes I feel that God laughs, yes. God laughs at all of these heated absurdities He puts into our bodies. He laughs at us all, Father. I am quite certain He laughs at you, Father, unable to take a woman in order to glorify His name with the mortification of your body—He must think that is a clever joke, that is. Father, I am filled with fevers of the flesh and I am shivering with heat, Father, and I am quite certain that you are a bigger fool than even I am and surely, to think this is sacrilege. I don't know. Is such a thing forgivable?"

The silence on the other side of the screen is complete. She cannot even hear the priest shifting around. She tries to listen for his breathing, some sign of life. Perhaps he has fainted dead away? It is possible that their wearing dresses gives priests fragile female constitutions, and their delicate ears cannot process such ignoble gushings of sin without draining all blood and cognizance out of their brains.

No, the man of God is here, and he is sentient. His gravelly disembodied voice speaks, finally: "Everything is forgivable, my child, if you have faith."

When Louise hears this, something in her heart startles so fiercely that she gasps. She realizes that these are the same words the priest spoke at her last confession. To both these queries, he dispenses the same noncomfort! She could storm into his side of the booth and rip the white collar from his throat and fling it at his face, that ridiculous bastard.

The repeated words close a circle in Louise's heart. Somehow, this strikes her as magnificent. It is like the sun's first rays blazing over the cold horizon. It is like a man tripping on a banana peel and falling face-first into a pie. It is stupid and hilarious. So she laughs.

Full-throatedly and without shame, Louise laughs and laughs and she stands up and goes out of the booth, leaving the priest there stymied, unable to dispense his penance. On her way out of the church and all the way to the metro station to take the train back home, she shudders with helpless mirth, knowing precisely what she wants to do next. It concerns a key, and a secret, and needing to get some air.

THE TRAIN PLOWS INTO the narrow subterranean darkness, bearing her toward home. The wheels and gears count out a metallic beat, while the rails wail like a glacial wind trying to sneak into the cracks of a shut door. The sound is difficult to listen to: the pitch is high and loud, and sad.

Louise is looking at a man standing by the door, presumably waiting to get off at the next stop. He is wearing a black suit, the jacket off and doubled over his arm. She likes his face: it looks dreamy in a boyish way, despite the fact that he must be at least in his forties, as indicated by the graceful sweeps of gray arcing over each ear, contrasting sharply against his black hair. There is something sweet and familiar about him; she almost wants to greet him, though she doesn't know him. The expression of his mouth is soft, almost like the whisper of a smile. His gaze is absorbed by the moving darkness beyond the window.

Louise wonders what he does for a living, and if he has a wife. She is about to look away from his face at his hands to see if there is a wedding ring, when the man winces suddenly, and falls to his knees. His bones hit the floor hard enough that the impact is audible, but the blankness of his stare doesn't change.

They are alone together in the train car, on this late weekday morning. It seems odd that there is no one else there. She must speak.

"Sir?"

The man doesn't collapse all the way down but merely sways there on his locked knees, his skin growing paler.

"Sir, are you all right?"

The partially fallen man parts his lips but says nothing. A tiny spot of blood begins to redden the immaculate whiteness of his tight shirt collar and it is then that Louise sees that he has begun bleeding from both his ears, in slow and delicate streams.

"Oh, God—Sir, please—what's the matter?"

What is happening? Is he going to die in front of her? Why today of all days?

She gets up, runs to the end of the train car, and in a blind flurry of panic pulls the alarm lever. The train stops immediately with a prodigious grinding of gears. At this lunge, the man topples. Louise runs to him and crouches next to him. She gathers his jacket and folds it under his head, to cradle it away from the grimy floor. His eyes are still open—can he see her?

They wait there. After a minute, the train conductor comes through the small door at the head of the car.

"What's all this?" he demands, as if the bizarre spectacle before him were just an inconvenience.

"I . . . I don't know," Louise stutters. "He just fell, and started bleeding from his ears. Something is very wrong."

The conductor is young, and wears a dapper navy jacket. He would be good-looking if it weren't for his pockmarked face. Louise is impressed that a metro conductor should look so dapper all by himself up there in his little cabin.

"Well—ah—well, I will have to take the train into the next station and there we will have to call an ambulance. All will be well, Madam; just stay as you are."

Louise nods, and watches the fellow jog back away and out of the train car. She can see that the people in the adjacent cars have gathered at the doors between the wagons to look through the glass at them, to see what is the matter. Still, no one comes in to help, as if they are afraid, or do not want to impinge on some sort of intimate moment.

And indeed it is an intimate moment that Louise shares with this stranger, holding his stricken body still and safe until help arrives. She wonders if the man is inside himself looking up at her, or if he is above looking down. Not that he is dead. She can plainly see his chest rise and fall, shallowly but without labor.[37] When his eyes close, it is as if he is going to sleep. Perhaps, while she enfolds him waiting for the paramedics to come take him, he dreams.

WHEN LOUISE GETS HOME, she does not waste a second. She swiftly packs a bag with a few of her clothes. She is breathing fast and deep.

---

37. Your face. As all fades to black and a strange hiss overtakes me, I cannot believe that I am looking at your face. The sweet concern in your eyes—if I could move I would reach my hand to touch your cheek. For an instant, a negative image of your eyes over the darkness then the thrum of my blood through my flickering brain then nothing.

Her heart pounds when she opens her jewelry box, as if she is afraid that the thing she is looking for is not there. It is. She slips the hidden key into the pocket of her overcoat. She goes into her husband's dresser and gets another key, this one to start up their motorcycle. This motorcycle they used to ride together on the country roads by his mother's house now resides in the courtyard downstairs, unused and covered by a tarp against the elements.

She can drive it. Henri has taught her.

She picks up her bag and is about to fly out of the apartment when she pauses for a moment. She finds the pad of mulch paper on which she writes her grocery lists. With a pencil, she scrawls:

Henri—

I am gone for a couple of days to get some air. I will return. I love you. I'm sorry.

Your wife,

Louise

She leaves this note for him on the dining room table.

Downstairs, in the courtyard, she tears the tarp off the motorcycle, leaving it lying in a crumpled heap on the ground. She flings her bag into the sidecar. She straddles the thing and starts it up hard, and laughs when it comes to life immediately beneath her.

To ride this roaring machine alone under the clear uniform sky—how lovely!

The journey will be long. At some point she will have to refuel. Probably her back will get sore and her ears will ring with the thundering of the motor long after she shuts it off. Just the same, she is not worried; she knows the way. She explodes out into the street more determined than she has ever been in her life to wind her way out of this all-encompassing and beautiful city, to find herself no-where, on her way to a place she is no longer welcome.

To trespass—without a doubt, one of her favorite crimes.

On her way out, she sees a streak of crimson on the edge of her dress sleeve. Oh, the stranger in the metro has bled on her a little. On this odd day, she wears his blood like an ornament, like a gift.

She thinks of the metro conductor, alone in his cabin all day, plowing into underground passages in a wailing machine full of faceless masses who never register his presence. He always sees darkness ahead, though he knows the shape of the path so well from taking it every day that his very body anticipates every curve of the rail. He is in numb harmony with it, and indeed the racket of the metro might even be a sort of white music to him.

Such is his daily work. He must have time to think. It musn't be so bad.

When she gets to her destination, she will not even bother to change out of her bloody clothes.

The speed does not make her dizzy, and she is not worried that she doesn't have a driver's license. She knows nothing will impede her journey, and no one will halt her. No one will even see her and stop to wonder what a lone woman could possibly be doing on a weekday morning flying out of Paris on a motorcycle, the blast of wind penetrating her buttoned coat and swirling around inside her dress, against her thrilled and shivering limbs.

That confounded girl, she thinks one last time, and decides to push her out of her mind for the duration of the trip, as Garance is not her biggest worry. Conception is on her mind now—the possibility of illegitimate life, unplanned and unknown but perhaps not unwelcome.

THE LINDEN TREES THAT line the path from the road to the house are much taller than the ones at the Palais Royal garden, unshaped by the trimming blades of a composition-minded gardener. Their leaves have mostly fallen. The clear, cold, blue sky is visible through their outreaching branches.

She pulls in and parks the motorcycle in the courtyard in front of the house. When she cuts the engine, the sudden silence is jarring. Her ears have to adjust to it like startled eyes swiftly subjected to darkness. Then the silence is wonderful: complete, unlike any of the moments of half quiet in Paris, where even the holiest cathedral is filled with shuffles and whispers.

The grass is green and lush everywhere, and quite overgrown. The new owners must not bother coming here much in the fall and winter months. The day is fresh and cloudless and seems to contain a harbinger of frost. Perhaps soon the unsheathed earth will be as hard as city asphalt.

The farmhouse, built of stone fitted together with packed earth, remains unchanged. She has always liked the red tile roof, despite the fact that some of the tiles are loose and have a tendency to get flung off during storms. As she walks to the door, she reaches in her coat pocket for the key she shouldn't have kept. She is nervous that the new owners have changed the locks; certainly that would be a reasonable precaution. But the new owners must be trusting people: the key fits and turns and all is well.

"Yes," she says softly to herself, "thank you."

LOUISE HELPS HERSELF TO the house. For the night, she takes sheets from a cupboard and makes one of the beds—a small one in a guest room. She is reluctant to take over the master bedroom of Henri's dead mother, though it has been settled since then by live people. Besides, sleeping in a small bed makes her feel like a child again, a child on an adventure. It suits her.

The sheets feel slightly humid and cold against her skin when she slips into them, but it doesn't matter. She soon falls into a dreamless, obliterated sleep.

THE NEXT MORNING, SHE feels inexplicably powerful, as if the property she is trespassing on is hers by some divine right. She takes a walk around the grounds. Her favorite place is the pond, black and still. The stream that runs into it is completely clear, and resumes its clear flow back out of the other end. It seems strange that the same water, when it is still, can be so opaque, so able to shield something from view.

It is colder today than yesterday, and Louise has to tuck her hands into her coat pockets to keep them warm. At the pond's edge, she flips a stone over with the tip of her shoe. The earth underneath is black and moist, and startled beetles skitter across it, suddenly exposed to the crisp air. Louise thinks of spring—of frogs leaping in the grass, moles burrowing in the ground, foxes sleeping in abandoned barns, insects swarming in every rotted tree trunk, sometimes even spiders in her bed. In the spring here, every spot bristles with delicate life. She thinks this would be a gorgeous thing to show a child: to catch a frog and cup it, to feel it palpitate in the palm of her hand, to touch its slick green skin and try to see its tiny amphibian soul through its globular gaze—to show her own child the simple wonder of live things.

What if this wish were granted to her? What if Xavier's seed had taken in her? It would be the most terrible wonderful thing that had ever happened to her. And her husband would suspect something, after all these years of infertility.

She mustn't make her stomach churn with foolish hopes and fears.

But what if he makes love to her again? It might happen then.

A new and dizzying future yawns open before her, as if the ground has cracked open at her feet. She has done a bad thing, but she cannot feel guilty: the possibilities are too exhilarating. She remembers Xavier's groan when he came, and a shiver of pleasure runs through her at the mere recollection.

She does not understand the power of that man's body over her. The image of his mouth especially flares up so vividly in her blood that she can't stand still—she has to resume walking immediately. He is like a poison in her, all the more potent because she doesn't want an antidote. She welcomes this disease of desire.

Surely this is a mark of her corruption, and surely she should feel ill over this, but she cannot. She feels wonderful and strong this morning. It occurs to her that she is famished, that she has not eaten in a long time. She decides to walk to the village and get something to eat, wondering idly if she will be judged for all the foolishness she has been indulging in lately. She has heard many times that life is a trial, and she has thoroughly internalized this notion, but she thinks it doesn't matter anyway: life is a trial that inevitably ends in an execution.

So why not commit a few harmless little crimes?

THE SILENCE IS UNNERVING and the darkness is complete. Tonight Louise cannot sleep without Henri's regular breathing next to her, without the sound of cars passing in the narrow street below and the moving yellow glow of their headlights. There isn't a speck of light or noise—only a vague smell of mold. Louise sits up in bed and looks around. The stillness brings her a random memory, flitting forward like a moth to a light.

A few summers ago, Henri's mother had bought a baby duck at the Sunday market, just to have a little someone swimming around the pond. The duckling, looking for parental figures, became attached to the chickens in the yard. Since he looked enough like a chick (small and yellow and downy), the chickens loved him back. He pecked happily for feed at their feet.

When Henri and Louise came to visit, they found the old woman angry at her duck, who had by then grown white and feathered with a long neck, like a small goose. The duck was not fulfilling his duck duties: he would not go near the pond. The chickens had taught him to be afraid of the water.

"This is ridiculous," she'd grumbled at her son. "Aren't these animals supposed to have an instinct for the water?"

Henri shrugged. "Instinct? We've bred flying out of these farm ducks. But he can probably be taught to swim."

"How's that?"

"We can fling him in a few times. He'll figure it out."

She laughed at this suggestion, having not thought of something that simple. Anyhow, it was a sound idea, so she told him to do it.

The duck was trusting and let himself be scooped up by Henri, who walked to the pond carrying him under his arm like a small sack of potatoes. He then hoisted the duck with both arms and flung him into the water as hard as he could, landing him approximately in the middle of the pond. When the animal's body hit the water, he panicked extravagantly and paddled back in a great flurry of flapping flings, his webbed orange feet working so furiously that he nearly levitated above the surface.

How Louise had laughed with her husband and his mother at the duck's refusal of his nature, at his mad scramble for safety and his total bewilderment.

It took quite a few flingings for the duck to understand that he belonged in the water. He eventually grew placid and confident there, bobbing along and diving to eat whatever it is that ducks eat in the secret murky depths. He was happy, having learned the place he belonged, but he was never again quite so trusting. He always ran away whenever anyone tried to pick him up.

After Henri's mother died, the duck was sold along with the chickens to a neighboring farmer.

Henri—how will Henri react when she comes home? He'll have to react; he'll have to say something. He ought to get angry. She tries to picture him that way, and cannot remember the last time she heard him raise his voice. What if they have an argument? What if he turns beet red and screams, demanding an explanation? Louise almost looks forward to that, to his infuriated eye gleaming with passion. What if she screams back and runs to the kitchen and starts throwing dishes on the floor? She wonders how he would react if she burst into tears in front of him. If he burst into tears in front of her, she simply wouldn't know what to do with herself—no, such a thing would never happen. Impossible.

For all that, if he guessed how she had defiled their marriage, some intensity of feeling would likely be wrung from him.

Yet she is not entirely sure that she has defiled the marriage, her mind cannot gain purchase on what she has done. Her grip slips. Her marriage is the structure on which her entire life rests, like a tectonic plate. She's gone and made an earthquake, even if Henri never feels its aftershocks. Maybe it's a good thing: maybe this release of energy has prevented some larger disaster in the future.

Still, in life, she is primarily Henri's wife, and she has clearly failed that function. She ought to feel low, and for the first time, she is beginning to.

Louise gets out of bed and puts her shoes on her bare feet, and her black coat over her nightgown. She goes and stands outside. It is much colder than it was during the day; the freshness of the air cuts into her lungs. She listens to the quiet, straining to hear a noise. She can make out rustlings in the grass that are so slight that she is unsure whether they are her own fancy. The sky is a perfect black, speckled with more stars than Louise remembers ever seeing. She gets a slight crick in her neck looking up at them.

Her marriage has made her know herself. If she is a cliff face at the edge of the ocean, then marriage is the water washing over her, shaping her through the years. This erosion uncovers hidden things in the rock: A vein of quartz, glittering in the sun. An unexpected fissure, now even more threatening to her structural integrity for being uncovered.

The water has worn her down and some part of her has dissolved away into the ocean, never to be seen again.

Tomorrow morning she will leave. She will pack her bag and make sure she leaves everything in the house as she's found it. She will strip the bed, fold the sheets, and put them away, secretly pleased that she is leaving her scent in them—leaving her mark on this place if only until the next time they are washed—and that no one will ever know this. She will even leave one of the bedroom doors slightly ajar at the same angle she first pushed it open from. She will lock the front entrance behind her and slip the key she shouldn't have kept back into her coat pocket. She will walk to the motorcycle backwards, in order to look at the house, the dark pond, the lush grass, for as long as possible.

Jouir comme ça

LOUISE GETS HOME IN the middle of the afternoon, determined to cook her husband a beautiful meal. She will light candles. She will speak softly and tell him how much she loves him. She might even tell him of what happened with Garance, to explain her disappearance, her need to get away to think for a while. Saying anything about Xavier Langlais is, of course, out of the question. She cannot tell if she is at a beginning or at an end with that man. How will she keep herself sane with him living in the apartment below hers? What if, one quiet night, she hears him make love to his wife? It seems then that the walls around her should fall to pieces as her throbbing brain bursts asunder, like an overripe fruit.

The notepad she has left on the dining room table hasn't moved. Her note is still there, untouched. Except—below it, Henri has made his own addition, also jotted hastily in pencil:

Henri—

I am gone for a couple of days to get some air. I will return. I love you. I'm sorry.

Your wife,
Louise

Louise—

Your leaving like this with no explanation and no word on when you will return has made it impossible for me to stay in this apartment for the time being. I cannot sleep here alone. I have gone to stay a few days with Pierre. If you come home and find this, you may fetch me there. In any case, I will return before the end of the week. I wonder if you will be here waiting?

I wish I knew what is happening.

I am angry. I think that I love you too—you will have to tell me who it is that I love. Explain.

Your husband,
Henri

Henri is angry! Will he still be angry when she sees him? What will he look like then? Should she go to him at Pierre's house? What does Pierre think about all this? What if her father knows she's left? Louise can see the three men around her, like a stern tribunal, questioning her hurtful flightiness.

She will not cook a beautiful dinner for tonight. She must go to Cleper's house to fetch her husband immediately. She is about to put her coat back on when there is a knock at the door—such a small knock that she might not have heard it had there been more ambient noise. She thinks maybe it's Garance come back to talk to her, to ask her why she wasn't there for their scheduled lesson. When she opens the door, Xavier is standing there, looking disconcertingly like an expectant boy.

"Why didn't you ring the doorbell?" she asks.

"I . . . ," he stammers. "I didn't want to disturb the peace? Your husband isn't home, is he?"

"No."

"Good."

She lets him in, closing the door quietly behind him. He has a high flush on his face, indicative of some sort of emotion, but otherwise he looks fairly inscrutable to her. He might be here to make love to her again; he might be here to tell her he must never make love to her again. She simply asks, "Why are you here?"

"Because I want you squirming under me, pinned down. Because I want to hear your voice quaver while you ask me to fuck you. Where have you been these past few days?"

"Ah," is all she finds to say. They are both flustered, as if they have been driven to this moment not entirely under their own volition—as if possessed but still enough themselves to be embarrassed about it.

"Oh dear." He sighs. "You know too much about me."

She laughs, gently touching his reddened cheek. "You are sweet, after all."

"Is that what I am?" he says as he grabs her by the waist and gives her one of his long, womb-quaking kisses. He backs her out of the entryway in the direction of the bedroom, working her dress up over her legs and caressing the warm skin of her thighs above where the garter belt meets the stockings. They leave a trail of her clothes across the living room, kissing all the while as if they are sucking life itself from each other's tongues. They cannot make it to the bedroom. Louise has to drop to her knees immediately, unbuckle his belt, open his pants, and suck his cock.

When it throbs in her mouth, it releases a tiny bit of semen, and Xavier gasps and pulls out. He grabs Louise by the shoulders, turns her around, and takes her on the floor, from behind, in front of the mirror that hangs on the door leading to her bedroom. Louise can see her own face there, transformed by arousal—her eyes dark and unfathomable, her lips as red and swollen as her cunt. From the first thrust, Xavier penetrates her so deeply that she cannot stop quivering—why is it, oh why is it that her body must yield so immediately and so completely to this man who came from nowhere?

. . . on the chair next to her dresser, on his lap facing him, his arms around her. He smothers her cries with his kisses. He stands up, still holding her. She squeals and clings to him, to his broad shoulders. He is so deep inside her, there is nothing but him in the whole world. He holds her there and she is amazed; her husband has never done this to her. Xavier carries her to the bed and falls on it with her, on top of her. Her juices drench them both. As he begins to thrust again, he speeds up his rhythm—

"Oh, Xavier . . . ," she gasps.

He moans in response. She can feel his cock quiver; he is going to come; she is going to die.

"Louise—yes, oh, Louise . . ."

When he says her name like that, his voice ragged as he takes his pleasure of her, she comes so hard that she could faint.

———

AFTERWARD, AS HE HOLDS her, she wants to say *I love you,* but she cannot. It would be too ridiculous. Instead she says, "You drink a lot of coffee."

"Maybe so; why do you say that?"

"Your semen   it tasted a bit like coffee."

He looks into her face, and she swears she can see tenderness in his clear blue eyes—which is so much more alarming than the former blankness there, and so much more wonderful. He responds, bemused. "There's an observation I haven't heard before! You're something else." Then he suddenly becomes very earnest when he declares, "I've never seen a woman come like that."

"How do you mean?"

"Come so much, I mean."

Louise is utterly disquieted by this pronouncement. She wonders about those other women he'd been with—how did they come, exactly? It strikes her as odd that she knows so little about her own sex. Are other women daintier about it? More restrained? Was her enthusiasm somehow indecorous?

"That's not bad, is it?" she asks tentatively.

"Good Lord, no. It's lovely. My hot, moist jungle creature—you are my Florida flower."

"So I will drive you mad and swallow you whole, will I?"

"That is entirely possible, and might be entirely pleasant. I just hope my wife didn't hear any of that!"

His wife—oh, his wife is just below them! She'd forgotten. She looks so stricken at the thought that he tells her not to worry, that he's certain the moans didn't travel down through the floor.

After all, he has never heard her with Henri. Louise has a moment of near mortification at that observation, but instead decides to hit him with her pillow and laugh. "Well, I will make sure to make more of a ruckus next time!"

AFTER XAVIER LEAVES, SHE does not have the stomach to go fetch her husband at Pierre's house. She does not have the stomach for anything, not even a light dinner. She feels ill and shivery, downright feverish. She suspects she picked up a cold on her excursion to the country. She makes herself a tisane before bed and sits bundled in blankets, letting the soothing herb-scented steam rise to her face from her cup before she takes her first sip, attempting to understand how it is possible for her to be so happy and so unhappy at the same time.

Paris

June 6th

Dear Sir,

It has been a while since I've written you; I am sorry. I have been in the hospital. One day on my way to work, I fainted in the metro. There was a swirl of activity around me, and some woman knelt on the floor and tucked my jacket under my head, holding me there until the train pulled up at the next station, where they would call paramedics for me.

Unable to speak or move, unable to hear anything except a crackling hiss like a detuned radio, all I could do was look up into the woman's face as she looked down at me, and the woman's face was this face:

I would have given anything to be able to speak, but I could not move a muscle while my eyes faded to black, though I could swear they were wide open. I felt a wave of feverish trembling radiate through all my limbs from my solar plexus, then nothing. Total obliteration, as if my body had flung out my very soul. There were no dreams, and when I woke up the next morning, I had no idea where on earth I was, or even who I was. I stared at the ceiling for entire minutes, gathering myself, gathering the information that paramedics back home ask of those who have been stricken to make sure they are still inside themselves: my name, the date, the identity of the current president. What was most strange about my predicament is that physically I felt absolutely fantastic—better than I had in many years. I felt strong, as if I owned the whole world. I felt that I could walk striking the ground with my heels as if it would crack beneath me. Everything felt crisp, and I was ravenously hungry.

The doctors seemed not to believe me when I explained to them that I was very well and that I wanted to go home. They cited the fact that I suffered a bizarre symptom when I fainted on the metro: I bled from the ears. They took a thousand scans and tests and squinted at images of my brain intensely in their doctorly fashion, looking for the source of my ailment. But there was no ailment. Even my fevers, which had haunted me for months, had completely abated. They kept me under observation and asked me many questions to make sure I was quite well, and sane. In order to convince them of the latter, I had to omit from my answers many of the things that have been happening to me lately.

I am quite sane. It is not 1928. I did not look up into Louise Brunet's long-dead face when I fainted in the metro. I do not feel a strange extraneous sentience in my flesh, permeating my blood, flowing through me while it laughs softly at me. Softly like an amused parent watching the blunderings of a child before gently setting the child straight.

For over two weeks I avoid the record; I avoid Josianne, even. I proceed normally with my life. I shuttle between my apartment, my office, the library. I am absorbed by my more suitable studies. I do not at all miss the magical touch and breathtaking kisses of my trickster goddess. I am not in the least gnawed by curiosity about the documentation; it does not eat my dreams. I do not gingerly lift the lid of the box and move its contents about with unsteady hands. I do not pick up a delicate, beautifully wrought pair of sewing scissors and slip my fingers through the small oval grips, opening the tiny, sharply pointed blades as if I am about to cut a thread.

The snip of the scissors is barely audible as I close them again, and the thread falls away from them airily, as light as snow. It is a frigid morning in the waning days of the year 1918; the hands wielding the scissors are a woman's hands; the eyes glancing back at me from the mirror on the wall are the same eyes that looked down at me after I'd fallen on the metro. Briefly they flit away, then back—how stunningly seamless this is: I am Louise Brunet, and there is no fever in my body. The fever is even gone from my brother's body: he has died mere minutes ago. I am sitting at the dining room table with my father and the priest who administered the last rites. I am sewing a fallen button back on my father's shirt, paying close attention to my slow work because I cannot bear to glance at either of them. The war is over and still he is dead and

I feel nothing. His skin is as white as the sheets he is tangled in, his blood is cooling, and soon his eyes will begin to sink slightly in his head. His face will be unrecognizable, a collapsed relic of his former self, and through the hours of the wake I will hardly be able to stand looking at it—this empty husk, my brother?

The three of us sitting here around the dining table my mother chose when she married, in this pregnant silence. . . . My father is staring into the middle distance, glowering, and the priest looks uneasy, as if the ire is aimed at him personally. He feels compelled to say something he thinks will be comforting, and as soon as the words come out of his mouth, I know they are a mistake:

"I know this is very difficult and I am very sorry for it, but we must learn to offer up our sufferings to the Lord."

My father stands up abruptly as if on springs, and I have never seen a look on his face such as he has now. He is distorted with beaming crimson fury, more terrible even than when he forbade my marriage to Camille. He nearly growls, "Your Lord is a vile, piteous joke. Your Lord should have taken him before leaving him for four years in the trenches, if taking him too soon for no good reason was his grand plan."

"Suffering cleanses us," the priest attempts. There could not possibly have been a more wrong thing to say, and my father moves against this pronouncement with striking-snake speed. He snatches up my sewing scissors and clenches them, with the small sharp point jutting out from his fist. He raises his arm, and I gasp, "Father—"

Both of them turn their heads to look at me, as if I had addressed them both; yet I do not care about the priest. I can imagine my scissors protruding at a jaunty angle from the side of his neck, and this does not bother me at all. Let his blood gush down his cassock; in

all likelihood such a small blade could not inflict a lethal injury anyway. I just don't want my own father to lower himself to such an act
of violence, not today of all days. Today we are already all too low.

The priest opens his mouth to say something, but my father has
the good sense to interrupt him before the words come out; he says
in a trembling voice, "You will not say another word. You will leave
this house at once or I will shove these scissors into your throat, I
swear it."

The priest stands, stock-still, while looking at me with implor-
ing eyes, as if I were the one responsible for these proceedings. I
very gently shake my head no, and he thankfully shuts his mouth.
He backs out of the room, leaving my father and me alone, and as the
front door shuts behind him, I surmise that it will be a long while
before he sees our faces at mass. (Indeed it will be a long while before I see his face again, his placid dark eyes and the exploded capil-
laries on his nose. Then he will have the decency to pretend that he
doesn't recognize me as I gleefully feed him a false confession.)

My father's face is ghastly pale, his eyes lost and drowning. A
choked sound escapes him, and I realize suddenly that it's a sob.
In all my life, I have never seen my father weep. He is aware of this
also; he is still trying to hold it in. I go to him. I take his hand, still
clenched so tightly around my sewing scissors. Gently, I cup it. I
give a kiss to his white knuckles. I whisper, "Let go."

Slowly he opens his hand for me, as one making a willful effort
to unfurl his rigid musculature. When he presents the scissors to
me on his open palm, I take them and put them on the table. I can
see the reddened imprint of the tiny handle there in his sweaty skin,
speaking the furious pressure of his emotion.

"Oh Father . . ."

"Yes?"

"You weren't going to . . . you weren't really going to stab him, were you?"

"I was."

For an instant, there is something in me that wants to laugh. Perhaps we might have ended this moment collapsed in sad yet healing mirth, if a rictus hadn't seized his face, forcing hot tears to gush forth from his eyes. Oh—my father is crying in earnest now, and the heat of his grief and shame permeates the very air I breathe. He covers his face with his hands because he cannot bear me seeing him wrecked like this. His knees give out under him and he collapses back onto the chair; his smothered weeping is the worst sound in the world—worse even than the last breath of his only son. His broken feelings are such a shock to my system that it doesn't even occur to my body to weep also; my concern is entirely with him. I drop to my knees before him and take the handkerchief out of his breast pocket. I gently touch his hands with the tips of my cool fingers. His are hot and wet from his tears.

"Don't stifle yourself so," I say softly. "Just let it flow freely."

He obeys me and rests his hands on his lap. He lets me dab at his tears with his handkerchief, attempting to comfort him as if he were a child and I his mother. He tries to catch his breath, but I can hear his voice flood when he says to me, "Louise, Louise, you are the only thing I have left."

"And you are too, Father. You are the only thing I have left."

"Ah, I am not." He gently shakes his head and appears to be gathering himself. "You will have a husband, and children, and a whole life ahead of you."

"Then these things will be yours also."

His stricken face looks to be softening; to encourage this soften-ing, I say, "I love you."

He answers, "I love you," but there is a strange inflection in his voice when he says this. With his thousand-yard eyes lost to me, he adds almost inaudibly, "You look so much like her."

I am about to ask whom he means when the realization crush-es my throat like the pressure of a choking hand—he means my mother, the mother who lived only to give me light, the mother of whom he has not spoken since we were children, my brother and I. I am left there, lips parted on a smothered utterance, when my father encircles my shoulders with his arms and kisses me hard on the mouth.

deliver us—

I am in a swoon when he does this, a near faint. I raise both hands when he does this and I cannot know if this is me attempting to fight him off or this is a gesture of surrender, as if he has pointed a gun at me —

lead us not into temptation but deliver us from evil—
suddenly I feel as if I am watching this from a great height—

hallowed be Thy name Thy kingdom come Thy will be done—
from a great height—oh, Louise—if your mouth opens for his tongue, time will tear open and I will float out forever, a dried dead husk in the great black nothing—

hallowed be Thy name Thy kingdom come Thy will be done—
Louise, I cannot stay in your body while you do this. You cannot blame this on possession . . .

forgive us our trespasses as we forgive those who trespass against us—

Not by me, anyway.

Our Father who art in heaven, Amen.

By some prodigious effort of will, I fling myself out. Out and away. I float. Oh, be in your own body for a second—breathe.

My name is Trevor Neville Stratton. What happens next after Louise is kissed by her father is not in the documentation.

It is possible that she yields entirely to his kiss. It is possible that her body goes limp, and that her father holds up her weight as he stands up from the chair, and turns her around so that the dining table presses against the back of her upper thighs. It is possible that he hoists her up and pushes her back on this table, parting her legs and pressing himself against the heat of her as he grows hard, readying himself to take his daughter the way a man usually takes his wife.

It is possible that she breaks away from his kiss. It is possible that she gasps in horror and puts her hand up to her sullied lips before turning from him and running away before he can say a word. It is possible that she locks herself in her room and cries for hours, cries so hard that she vomits into a trash can, hoping to God that He will obliterate the soul-rattling memory of this kiss the way He seems to like obliterating everything else.

I cannot know; I am not her.[38] I can merely conjecture because such singular occurrences are not in the record.[39]

---

38. Am I certain of this?

39. However, this much is known: that evening, he goes to Louise and finds her

40

bedroom door locked. He knocks on it gently. At first she does not answer. He knocks again. "Yes?" answers her raw, tear-soaked voice.

"Open up, please."

She does, because she is an obedient daughter, but she stands in the open door-way, afraid to so much as let him see her unmade bed, lest it invite him. Her face is swollen from too much weeping. He thinks, The poor child, this is the worst day of her life. "Will you be all right?" he asks.

She nods silently, and she even manages to smile, just a little. How is she doing that? She is so strong. He says quite softly, with all the gentleness of a courteous suggestion, "I think it would be good if you should marry."

"I can't imagine to whom."

"That fellow from my shop, Henri Brunet. He likes you."

Louise casts her eyes down, and he can tell he has said enough. He does not, after all, want to push his daughter. He doesn't have to. His observation, to her, has the strength of an edict. He says good night, and she shuts the door. At the sound of his retreating footsteps, she recalls the outrage with which he greeted the idea that she might marry her own blood when Camille asked him for her hand, and she could laugh hysterically until her heart completely crumbles, never to be mended again. Fortunately he is dead now. They are all dead.

40. How is this much known? There is nothing in the documentation that so much as insinuates this. I am ridiculous.

I am

No Where (help me!)[41]

41.

But this is no help at all! It is a photograph of Louise Brunet at an advanced age. It is dated 1956. She is standing next to her elderly father, who died of a massive heart attack in 1944. He is standing next to her plump mother, who died when she was born. This cannot be! This cannot be in the documentation—don't fall apart

don't fall apart

no no don't fall apart

please.

My name is Trevor Stratton and today is—uh—

Calm yourself, Trevor. Still your tremor.

My name is Trevor Neville Stratton and today is—

D.Q. le 4	**Novem.**	N.L. le 12		P.Q. le 20	**1928**	P.L. le 27
1 Jeu	TOUSS			16 Ven	Edme	
2 Ven	Trépa.			17 Sam	Aigna.	
3 Sam	Hubert			18 Dim	Claudi	
4 Dim	Charl⁰			19 Lun	Élisab.	
5 Lun	Bertil⁰			20 Mar	Edmo.	
6 Mar	Leona.			21 Mer	P.N.D.	
7 Mer	Ernest			22 Jeu	Cécile	
8 Jeu	sᵗᵉRel.			23 Ven	Clème.	
9 Ven	Mathu			24 Sam	Flore	
10 Sam	Juste			25 Dim	Cather	
11 Dim	ARMIS			26 Lun	Delph.	
12 Lun	René			27 Mar	Severi.	
13 Mar	Brice			28 Mer	Sosth.	
14 Mer	Philoᵉ			29 Jeu	Satur.	
15 Jeu	Eugèn.			30 Ven	André	
Les jours diminuent de 1 h. 23.						

Today is

a Friday in the middle of an unusually warm November in the year
1928. This is what the book tells you, the same little book that Louise marked with an X on June 19, and another X precisely one month
later. Her period had been due on June 19, which she realized with
much trepidation a few days later when it didn't come. The hope of it
was a strain to her: Could it be after all this time? A happy accident?
She watched her body, waiting for nausea, or tender breasts, or any
sign. It told her nothing. Then on July 19, blood came—a great deal
of it, with much pain. She suspected that perhaps the gush was not

late menses but an early miscarriage; it didn't matter, the result was the same. It was not even worth mourning this nonexistent incipient life. Still, the idea of it rippled through her and left its mark: the two Xs bracketing her month of foolish hope, the only days she singled out in Cleper's little calendar.

This morning, on Friday, November 16, the rising sun is attempting to pierce a misty morning, and Louise hovers in a space in between. She cannot tell whether she is asleep or awake, but she is quite certain the illness that was beginning to manifest the previous night is now blooming fully upon her. She is burning and freezing at the same time; her half-formed thoughts race so fast through her head that she cannot gain purchase on any of them. As her limbs tremble, she is enveloped by a roar. At first it sounds like the rushing of water, but eventually it resolves into a crackling hiss with jumbled voices in it, something like a radio with several stations coming in at once. The voices resolve into a chorus—

C'est la Carmencita.

Non, non, ce n'est pas elle . . .[42]

The fever surges and Louise's entire body twitches. She whimpers. All the muscle fibers inside her are wound so tightly that she is afraid that they will start snapping one by one, infinitesimally tearing her apart.

L'amour est un oiseau rebelle
que nul ne peut apprivoiser—[43]

---

42. *It's Carmencita.*
    No, no, it is not her . . .
43. *Love is a wild bird*
    that none can tame—

A flower is tossed by a slowly arcing arm, serpentine and suggestive. Louise is suddenly so hot that she throws her covers off.

Si il y a des sorcières,
cette fille-là en est une.[44]

The flower is infinitely delicate. A breath of wind could cruelly rip off its soft, tender petals (no, no, don't fall apart), and there is a burst of electricity in the hollow under Louise's heart.

(please)

"Louise?"

At the sound of her name, her eyes pop open. There is someone in the room, someone with a male voice—an unfamiliar male voice. She struggles to cover her pale bare legs with a sheet and looks across the room to see me, sitting on the wooden chair her husband usually puts his discarded clothes on when he undresses at night. Her eyes grow wider as a violent flush overtakes her face.

"You!" she says. "You don't exist!"

I answer as softly as possible, "I beg to differ."

"How did you get here?"

"Same way I always do." As I say this, I raise the small object I am holding in my hand, the same one she currently has on her nightstand: a small rectangular cardboard box containing ribbon with her initials on it, to be cut up and sewn inside her clothes so that they do not get mixed up when she sends her laundry away to be cleaned.

---

44. *If witches exist,*
    this girl is one.

[NB:]

I notice a familiar object next to the little green box on her night-stand—the same box I am holding. I have seen these sewing scissors before. Surprised at seeing them sitting there looking so quotidian and innocent, I exclaim, "You still use them?"

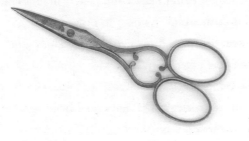

[NB:]

"Yes, why not? What do you mean?"

"That day . . . when your brother died—that day with the priest?"

"They weren't sullied with the priest's blood. They are perfectly fine scissors."

She sits up laboriously in bed, propping her back up against the headboard with a pillow. "So you know about that day." She sighs. "Of course, you were there."

I am about to answer her in the affirmative when she laughs hys-terically, as if someone has told her a joke as hurtful as it is funny. I am a bit flummoxed by this display. As she wipes the tears beading at the corners of her eyes, she hoots, "But of course you were not there! You aren't even here! I am delirious with fever."

"You are. You are burning up."

She is suddenly serious—a very mercurial woman in her delirium. She stares at me with her shining eyes and says simply, "It was you my brother saw, the day before he died."

I nod.

"I am going to die from this fever, then. You are the one who comes to fetch us when we die."

"Oh no! I am no such thing. My name is Trevor Stratton. I am just an academic. I do research."

"I am—your research?"

"In a manner of speaking."

"I am going to die tomorrow."

She says this with some degree of distracted bemusement in her voice, as if she has discovered an incongruity in the fabric of life. I am in a fluster now, because condemning people to death is certainly not what I do. "I assure you that is not so. You will be fine. Look," I say as I root around in my pocket and pull out a small photograph, "Xavier will take this of you and Pauline next week, on an outing in the public garden."

[NB: ⁴⁵]

She holds out her hand for the picture and I briefly wonder if some anomaly will result from her seeing it now, from looking at her future face. Am I not supposed to do that? Well, this entire situation violates space-time in plenty of ways already, so I decide it can't do that much harm and I let her snatch the photo from me.

"Ha!" she exclaims. "The picture looks old."

"It is."

She is utterly fascinated by it, and scrutinizes it intently for a full minute. "Well, I will make sure to smile for such a momentous picture. You see I already have. We're not too bad-looking, no?

---

45. Properly captured for the record: the gaze of Xavier Langlais, a man illegible, not in the documentation.

That's a funny hat she will have on, though. Do you like my hat? It's my favorite one."

"The purple one?"

"So you know the color too. It seems you know everything. So tell me, Mr. Stratton, when will I die?"

"That information is not in the documentation."

"Ah. When will my father die, then?"

I could answer, if I wanted to. I could tell her. But there is something wrong with that. I repeat as firmly as I can manage, "That information is not in the documentation."

"You are very spooked by death, for a man who doesn't exist."

"It gets us all."

A slight smile is playing on her dry pink lips, as if after all she finds me amusing. I am glad for it. After all, as anyone, I just want to be liked. For a sick woman, the words are coming out of her with ease—but of course we have all grown familiar with the strange and unexpected qualities of these fevers. She hands me the picture back, asking, "You know the man who will take this picture?"

"Yes."

"You know what he is to me, then?"

"Of course. I have been in his body. I have been in all your bodies."

"Wait, were you in his body when he was in my body?"

"That is a great deal of possession, isn't it?"

"Quite. Will I have his child?"

She is so earnest when she asks me this question, so childlike and eager herself. She does not ask me: How long will he be my lover? Will my husband find us out? Will his wife? Am I a bad person for doing this? Having me before her, her oracle, she wants to know: Will I have his child? The hope in her voice pains me, for there isn't a single child of hers in the record. The child is a vaporous dream, never to be. Can I tell her that? We are not supposed to know that, are we—that we will not have the thing we most want? That is the sort of thing that erodes souls. That is the sort of thing one must find out in the fullness of time. Oh, for the love of all that is good and true, I must lie.

"That is not yet determined."

She laughs, more good-naturedly than I deserve: "Truly, you are an oracle! Oracles always spout gibberish, answer questions with other questions, and refuse to say anything definite. You must contain the wisdom of the ages."

Now it is I who turn red, the blood rising to my face from embarrassment and irritation. Why breach the order of history if I have nothing important to give her from this exchange? I must give her something. Without thinking I blurt out: "I was in Camille's body too."

"You were—oh—," she gasps. Tears glimmer in her eyes over the film of fever as she whispers, "What did you see?"

Why did I say that? What am I to answer? I was in him when he did dreadful things to a German boy, when he was hardly more than a boy himself. I saw him suffer and unwind. I saw him die. My lips part to answer, but I do not speak. The look on my face must be very eloquent because Louise asks gently, "You saw him die?"

I nod.

"How did he die? You must tell me."

My mouth is still open on silence when she says, "Oh, he suffered terribly. I can tell just from your face."

"Yes. It's over now, Louise."

"Trevor, where was he shot?"

"In the back, out through the gut."

"It hurt very much."

"Yes."

"And he was conscious for it."

I do not have to answer; the gaze we exchange is enough. "He saw you," she whispers almost inaudibly.

"Yes; he saw the canceled envelope from your last letter to him too. He wanted me to tell him what you'd written him."

Her eyes widen, and I cannot tell whether the sheen of sweat on her pale face comes from terror or the fever that grips her body. She pulls the covers over her torso as if to protect herself when she says, "It is impossible for you to have that letter. It is destroyed."

"What we are doing now is impossible," I observe, then hasten to add, "but you're right. I don't have that letter. It is not in the record."

"Did you tell him you didn't have the letter?"

"No. I didn't tell him that. I didn't have the heart to tell him that in the state he was in, in his last moments. You can imagine that, can't you?"

"Yes, but then what did you do? You had nothing to read him."

"I did what I always do. I falsified."

"You wrote a fake letter? From me?"

"Yes. It was very loving."

"You wrote a fake love letter. From me." She says this absently, looking through me as if I am transparent, which for a moment makes me suspect that I am beginning to vanish. She appears grieved but peaceful. Her moist eyes glisten in the shadow and a smile passes on her face, so small that it is nearly imperceptible. Before I can speak again, she looks at me fixedly and says, "It seems you and I have a bit in common."

"It seems so."

"You did good, Trevor. Thank you."

"I try."

"Are you feeling anything in your body right now?"

"Only a great weariness. Why?"

"You are fading. And I feel the weariness too. I will be asleep soon."

"And when we awaken, we will think we dreamed this."

"No—take something with you."

"What?"

"Take something back with you, from this room. And give me something before you go. So that we can remember it was real."

"What shall I take?"

Quicker than I thought a woman in a sickbed could move, Louise reaches for her nightstand and plucks up the tiny box of label ribbon lying there. She presents it to me on an open palm. I hesitate: "The same artifact that brought me here? If I take it back with the one I already have, does that not violate some law of the universe?"

"Isn't that grand? I want to see if the universe collapses when you leave here."

"It is likely that the universe will determine a way to go on," I answer as I take the object from her hand and tuck it into my breast pocket along with its duplicate, next to my fluttering heart.

"Likely. Now give me something. Some piece of you."

I consider giving her the picture of herself with Pauline, but that is a piece of her, not of me—and, besides, life will give her this artifact itself in a week's time. I can feel myself disappearing, so in a fluster I invert both my trouser pockets, looking for anything that might be there. I am startled by the sonorous, clear ring of something hitting the ground. The sound galvanizes me into picking the item up and presenting it to her:

"See?" I say. "A bit of stray cash."

She laughs and answers, "If I'd known all you men were going to keep throwing that pun back at me, I would have thought of a better one."

"It is perfectly suited for our purposes."

"Essentially meaningless, you mean."

"Just so," I answer as she looks over the dime with great interest, tilting it into the weak winter morning light streaming in through the window. "You are an American," she observes. "I thought your accent was British."

"Yes, American."

"You are from farther than I thought," she says as she flips the coin, then bursts into laughter when she sees the date it will be

struck[46]—   "a lot farther than I thought!"

---

46. 1967, from my perspective an old coin.

"Do you like it? I'm glad that happened to be in my pocket to mark this day."

"Yes, it's wonderful. Tell me, who is that man?" she asks as she displays the dime to me. Without thinking, I answer, "He was the president of—oh, dear me."

It occurs to me that the man in question will not be the president of the United States for nearly five more years. Is it possible that such an anomalous object will remain with her after I am gone? I reach out to lay my finger on the coin in her hand, but my hand passes through hers with no contact. Soon I will be gone, but my little memento will stay: I pass through it; it does not fall through her.

"He will be the president of the United States!" I shout, as I would over a failing telephone connection.

"Thank you!" she shouts after me, as my vision darkens to black and a roar like interference drowns out her voice. Before I lose consciousness, I hear another voice, a woman's voice, ringing pure and true above the crackling confusion in my head:

Mais si je t'aime, si je t'aime, prends garde à toi![47]

A flower is tossed and I will sleep now.

[NB: I wake up fully clothed sitting up in my hard-backed desk chair, with the record sprawled out before me. There is no interim half-dream state: I am dropped most unceremoniously into full consciousness, as if from a great height. The back of my shirt is drenched with sweat as if I have made some tremendous effort with my body, but really I feel

---

47. *But if I love you, if I love you, you best beware!*

fine. I shove my hand into my breast pocket and I pull out the small green cardbox box of label ribbon that I put there before I lost myself and—

oh, fancy that!

Now there are two.

When I went to sleep in the middle of my research, there was only one, and now there are two. Most anomalous. To say the least, I feel a bit unwound. (My name is Trevor Stratton, and it is not 1928.)

A bit unwound (I am smiling now; I can't help it—this is entirely too loopy and wonderful for a reasonable man such as myself):

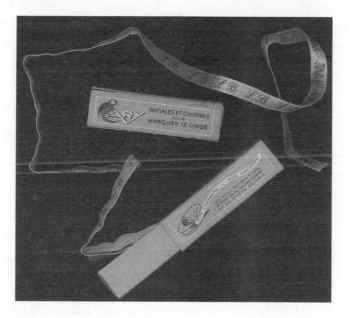

A bit unwound, yes.

With unsteady hands, I reach for the small box of change saved by Louise Brunet, stray cash that marks the important days of her life—even some that happened before she was born. The lid slides smoothly off, then I upturn the bottom half rudely onto my desk, the coins ringing loudly against the tabletop. With eager fingers, I root through them and I find— don't fall apart

(and why not after all?)
oh, how heartily I laugh—because there it is, a little piece of me embedded right here in the documentation,

an artifact saved from the future and preserved through time until the future is once more in the past	an artifact that I slipped into the box myself during a moment of monkey trickery that I cannot now recollect

but it is real

but I am a falsifier

but there is no way to know
unless you toss the coin

to find out
please.]

LOUISE IS WOKEN UP with a start by Henri's cool hand laid gently on her forehead. When she opens her eyes, she sees his weary concerned face looking down at her. She can see that he has just gotten home: his coat is still on. When he came through the front door and saw signs that she had returned, he didn't even bother taking it off before looking for her and finding her here asleep, tangled in sweat-dampened sheets.

"I was all set to be angry with you," he says, "but now you had to foil it all by being ill. Have you been like this long?"

"I'm sorry; you can be angry with me. I feel a lot better."

She realizes when she speaks these words that they are true: her fever has completely broken and now she feels fine—only a bit disoriented by the black, annihilated sleep she just had. She feels as if Henri has pulled her up suddenly from a pool of dark water, and she is still getting her bearings as oblivion slowly drips off her in the midday light. She looks around the room to make sure that the apparition from this morning is truly gone; she recalls him fading away bit by bit from his feet up, until only his eyes were left there, hovering—then nothing. When she blinks, she thinks she sees their white negative images still imprinted in her.

Henri pulls a chair up by the bedside and sits on it, the same one that the apparition had sat in. She would think that fellow a chimerical delusion, except she can see the strange little coin he left her still sitting on her nightstand. She will have to save that, to remember. Henri doesn't notice it; he is mainly concerned about one thing:

"Did you go away with a man?" he asks.

"No."

"You still love me, then."

"Yes."

"Why did you leave like that?"

Louise searches for a plausible reason through the lifting fog in her brain, and is overwhelmed by the surprising multiplicity of them. Why do we not leave all the time, after all? She sits up in bed and lifts her moistened hair off the back of her neck, to cool it. As she feels the movement of air against her tingling skin, she says, "You know that girl Garance? The piano student?"

"She came by while you were gone, looking in an awful fluster. She said she would come back this afternoon to see if you were here. That's why I returned now, to make sure that at least someone would be here to answer the door."

"Did she look scared?"

"I think. I'm not sure. Agitated. You left because of her?"

"That morning she came by and she gave me a pile of music she'd written for me. She told me she loved me and kissed me on the mouth. Quite thoroughly."

"She . . . what?"

"Exactly."

Henri processes this information for several seconds, as if attempting to reconcile it with what he previously knew of the girl. It seems to mesh, and he says, carefully, "That is . . . rather sweet, in a very strange way. That's why you went away, because Garance is in love with you? Where did you go?"

"I'm sorry. It wasn't rational. It might have been I was getting a little sick already, and somehow my mind was affected. I just felt as if I had to get out and get some distance, as if so many things were suddenly different. I just went to the country. I stayed in Bracieux."

"Oh. Did you go see the old house?"

"Yes."

She wants to tell him she stayed there, not at the inn in town as he assumes she did. She wants to tell him she still has the key, but somehow the words get stuck in her throat. She wasn't supposed to have made a copy—one of the many tiny transgressions she sprinkles throughout her existence to make it bearable for herself.

"It looks just the same, Henri. Everything is just the same."

"Do you want me to turn that girl away when she comes to see you today?"

"Dear me, no. Everything will be all right. You mustn't worry. I was just thrown for a bit, that's all. Does my father know I went away?"

"No, but Pierre does. He is quite convinced you went away with a man. He offered to track him with me and hold him down as I beat him up!"

For a moment, Louise pictures this scenario with Xavier and is about to be alarmed when she sees that her husband is smiling broadly, quite amused at the absurdity of the idea. "Imagine me beating someone up!" He chortles.

"Well, didn't you shoot people? During the war, I mean."

"Oh, Louise, you know we were all different during those times, like animals. We had to be."

She wishes she'd had the courage to be different back then, an animal. Instead she'd mistimed it and she became an animal just after the war ended, on the day her brother died. Now she is a breed meant to be errant, but constantly under confinement, always wiggling out of her restraints when nobody is looking. Poor Louise, being now what she should have been then and being then what she should be now: what an unfortunate mix-up.

"I saw something interesting on the metro ride back here," Henri says. "While the train was stopped at a station, I watched a woman come up to a man and ask him for a light. The fellow, who was smoking, said, 'It's funny you should ask that because I just got a light from someone else; I don't even have a match on me.' The woman with the unlit cigarette was about to walk away when the man said,

'Wait—here, you can light it off mine.' The two of them connected their cigarette tips and sucked. There was a small red flare-up as ignition took, and at this moment the train door closed the scene from me. We pulled away into the tunnel with a great grinding of gears and I left them there like that, exchanging this small kiss of fire. I will never see them disconnect. They could still be there on the platform, lighting each other up."

"Out of time. While the rest of us proceed."

"There is no way to know, is there?"

"That information is not in the documentation."

Henri laughs at this strange pronouncement from Louise, but does not find it out of place. Husband and wife feel relief at this moment, as if they have been through some great trial while they were apart, and now all will be well again. It is a moment of companionship. Louise reaches for Henri's hand, and he takes hers. For several seconds they gaze into each other's eyes, quite absorbed with observing each other, their fingers entwined. Louise sees how much they have both aged in nearly a decade together, how the peaks and hollows of their faces have softened and how time has etched fine lines into their skin. She is glad for it, for the record time makes in flesh and for the record bodies make in each other. She is glad for the heat of his hand against hers.

Without disconnecting his fingers from hers, Henri sighs and remarks, "You ought to get up and get dressed, Louise, and gird yourself. Garance will be here soon."

"Yes," she answers, "it's time to get back into the flow of things, isn't it?"

IT IS SO MUCH easier with Garance than she expects. The girl is so happy that Louise is back, and seems to feel no awkwardness. Since they can't manage to sit still while they talk about what Louise did while she was away, they take a walk together in the Jardin du Palais Royal. They stop at the flower patches and lean together on the fence that separates the tiny garden from the walkway, elbow to elbow. The plants are small and scraggly at this time of the year, green uninterrupted by any bloom.

"Look!" shouts Garance, pointing excitedly like a child half her age. When Louise glances where she's told, she is amazed. There is a solitary fragile flower unfurled delicately in one of the plants, a splash of color wavering tremulously in the cool afternoon breeze. It is a pansy, purple and white, an unexpected, daring offspring of this unusually warm November.

"That flower is crazy!" Garance says. "It will die immediately at the first frost. And still it tries."

"You know," Louise says without forethought while she looks at the girl's limpid green eyes and wind-pinkened cheeks, "the boy I loved during the war used to press pansies into his letters to let me know he was thinking of me."[48]

48. Like so: _____. Witness the ghost of the flower evident where Louise's lover writes, "Your cousin who loves you and thinks of you—Camille."

"Oh . . . it was . . . not Henri?" Garance asks gingerly.

"His name was Camille."

"What happened?"

"He died, of course."

"I'm sorry."

"It's all right. It was a long time ago."

"Sometimes time doesn't matter."

"That's true." Louise sighs. "How did you get to be so wise?"

"Must be all the music, I suppose." Garance shrugs, as if this connection is evident.

Louise laughs, delighted at the girl's matter-of-factness. "Well, aren't you dreadfully modest!"

Garance turns back to the flower. "Look at that bold little thing. Isn't it a shame that it will have to die before it withers on its own? It's already getting colder."

"Well, it should die for a cause, then," Louise proclaims as she leaps over the fence.

"What are you doing?" Garance squeals.

"I would like to have it," Louise answers breathlessly as she bends over quickly and plucks the flower with a sharp tug. Just as the stem breaks cleanly in her hand, she hears a shrill sound that almost knocks her out of her body.

"A gendarme!" Garance frets as she jumps madly in place, waving Louise on to leap back over the fence. "Run like hell!"

In a flash, Louise sees the angry man in his navy blue uniform running straight for her, his face a gleaming crimson as he puffs out his cheeks, blowing his whistle for dear life. She is in trouble with the authorities, yet the elation in her speeding heart makes her exploit take on an air of unreality, as if she is watching herself from a great height. She clambers back over the fence, much more awkwardly than the catlike bound she took over it the first time, still carefully holding the flower so as not to crush it. When she is safely over, she runs like hell, listening to Garance breathing fast and heavy between gusts of laughter as she runs beside her, neither looking back at the screaming man behind them.

The two of them shout in glee at the open blue sky together, Louise holding the fresh moist flower pressed neatly between her palms, her hands held flat against each other as if in prayer. She thinks of Xavier's mouth pressed against hers; she thinks of her brother making funny faces at her in church; she thinks of the woman who gave her life so that she could be here today trespassing and committing this small act of thievery; she thinks of the jumble of all the days before and all the days after, yet somehow there is only this moment, only this moment as she runs toward home with this giggling girl who loves her so, only this moment that she will have to somehow preserve, for the record.

Off the Record

*J*osianne is sitting at her desk quite bored when a clerk
from the mailroom comes up to her bearing an armload
of envelopes. He looks slightly irritated at having trudged up the
stairs for what he clearly considers an annoying errand. "Can you
give these to the American?" he says as he hands her a stack of large
yellow envelopes. "He never fetches his mail and his box is full."

"Certainly."

"Since I came all the way up here, I brought your mail too," he
announces gruffly as he drops a few small white envelopes on her
desk, then leaves without waiting for her thanks.

Josianne looks over the packets for Trevor. She is vexed with
him: he suddenly disappeared. After the love they made, once,
twice, three times—then he was gone. She is stricken, disappointed.
Is he scared? She wants to be indifferent to the packets waiting on
her desk for him, but they are too mysterious: six of them, of uniform size and heft, all addressed neatly to *Monsieur Trevor Neville
Stratton* at his office, bearing canceled stamps but no return addresses. There is something irresistibly compelling about them, as
if they are radiating some faint exhalation of strangeness, like exotic
objects brought from very far. She is usually not so nosy, but she is a

woman possessed by ravenous curiosity—and besides, why should she care if he is mad that she's opened his mail? She tears open one of the envelopes and pulls out the first page inside. The letter is addressed to a *Dear Sir* and signed . . . *Trevor Stratton*.

What sort of utterly bizarre man calls himself Sir? What sort of utterly bizarre man writes to himself and then posts himself his own letter, bothering to cancel a stamp and wait for it to come back to him?

The letters are all addressed to *Dear Sir*. They are all signed *Trevor Stratton*, except for the last one that trails directly off into the same sort of strange content that follows the other letters. When she flips through the text, it makes her smile in utter delight. It looks quite familiar to her, though of course she has never seen it before; she knows it like something that might have come to her in dreams. But where is his last signature? This bothers her. She skips through the entire packet to the last couple of pages and reads the following:

Off the Record

Paris, June

*J*osianne is sitting at her desk quite bored when a clerk from the mailroom comes up to her bearing an armload of envelopes.

What?

No.

The tricky monkey. He is even worse than she is! She loves him to pieces. The blood rushes madly around her heated body as she reads on, gripped by an elated vertigo. She skips down to the present moment and reads the following:

She skips down to the present moment and reads the following:

How do you like them? I wrote them for you. I think they belong to you a little, too. Don't worry, darling, I won't tell anyone you opened my mail. Come to me. I am in my office.

With love,

Trevor Stratton

Trevor Stratton

Afterword

When I was a little girl growing up in Paris in the early 1980s, an old woman who lived a few floors up from my apartment died alone. Her name was Louise Brunet. She had no remaining relatives to come fetch her belongings, so the landlord had to clear them all out. He let the other tenants in the building scavenge through her stuff and take home silverware, jewelry, whatever they wanted. My mother salvaged a small box filled with mementos: old love letters from WWI, mesh church gloves, dried flowers, a rosary—many objects worth nothing but memories. This box is the sepulchre of Louise Brunet's heart. The story behind the objects is lost; the objects are now the story.

As I have carried this strange box through life and across the world, I have always intended to make a book out of it. This book now exists; you hold it in your hands. The Louise Brunet depicted within it is a fiction; the real Louise Brunet is irretrievable. Still, she gave me the stars. I merely drew the constellations.

Use your smartphone's app to read the following QR codes and see enhanced versions of these images or go to www.13rueTherese.com.

page 9.

page 23.

page 28

page 32.

page 62.

page 74.

page 80.

page 83.

page 108.

page 113.

page 120.

page 123.

page 154.

page 160.

page 248.

page 261.

Acknowledgments

I am deeply indebted to Reagan Arthur, my editor, for her care and kindness with this novel. Thanks also to the great team at Little, Brown for all their hard work. I owe eternal gratitude to Bonnie Nadell, my agent, for her belief in my work and her guidance. And of course, oodles of love to Harris Shapiro, the best husband a woman could ask for.

About the Author

❖

Elena Mauli Shapiro grew up at 13, rue Thérèse in Paris, France. She has a BA in English and French from Stanford University, an MFA in Fiction Writing from Mills College, and an MA in Comparative Literature from the University of California, Davis. She currently lives in the Bay Area with her husband.